*A Candlelight
Ecstasy Romance*®

**"I THINK WE'D BETTER BREAK THIS UP . . .
UNLESS YOU WANT IT TO GO FURTHER," HE
SAID QUIETLY.**

"I don't know . . . what I want," she whispered. "I've
never been with anyone but Quinn."

Price chuckled and brushed his lips across hers again.
"You don't have to tell me that. But I know if you're
feeling what I'm feeling . . . six months is a long time." His
mouth took hers in another long, lazy kiss. "You say the
word. I think we could bring each other a lot of pleasure
tonight." He moved her closer against him.

Erin's thoughts were whirling. Price had awakened a
hungry need in her, one that had lain dormant for a long
time now. She had given herself in love to one man, only
to find heartbreak. How could she succumb to this man
she barely knew? How could she resist when her own
treacherous body had already promised more?

CANDLELIGHT ECSTASY ROMANCES®

OUT OF CONTROL

Lori Copeland

A CANDLELIGHT ECSTASY ROMANCE ®

Published by
Dell Publishing Co., Inc.
1 Dag Hammarskjold Plaza
New York, New York 10017

Dell ® TM 681510, Dell Publishing Co., Inc.

Candlelight Ecstasy Romance®, 1,203,540, is a registered
trademark of
Dell Publishing Co., Inc., New York, New York.

ISBN: 0–440–16751–5

Printed in the United States of America
First printing—May 1984

*To my editor, Lydia E. Paglio, for her marvelous patience
and understanding with a new writer.*

To Our Readers:

We have been delighted with your enthusiastic response to Candlelight Ecstasy Romances®, and we thank you for the interest you have shown in this exciting series.

In the upcoming months we will continue to present the distinctive sensuous love stories you have come to expect only from Ecstasy. We look forward to bringing you many more books from your favorite authors and also the very finest work from new authors of contemporary romantic fiction.

As always, we are striving to present the unique, absorbing love stories that you enjoy most—books that are more than ordinary romance.

Your suggestions and comments are always welcome. Please write to us at the address below.

Sincerely,

The Editors
Candlelight Romances
1 Dag Hammarskjold Plaza
New York, New York 10017

CHAPTER ONE

"Huntwey fwushed that ball down the toilet again!" Holly Daniels crossed her dainty five-year-old arms in an irritated stance and glared at her honorary aunt.

"Oh, Holly! Not again. Couldn't you have stopped him?" Erin closed her eyes in weary frustration, her headache growing steadily worse. Since she had arrived yesterday to baby-sit with the twins while her best friend, Brenda, and her husband fled gratefully on a well-earned vacation, Huntley had done his best to upset the normal routine of the household. If what Holly said was true, this would be the second time today that the monstrous other half of the adorable little girl standing before her had flushed a ball down the commode, then stood back in calm fascination to watch the water seep nastily over the white porcelain rim.

"*I* told him that plumwers don't come cheap now days," Holly said in a very adult miffed tone, only her lisping speech marring her image, "but he only *defied* me again!"

Erin put down the potato she was peeling for their dinner and tramped agitatedly down the hall to the twins' bedroom. The distinct sound of water overflowing in the small bath reached her ears as she stepped into the room. Huntley looked up from his perch in the middle of the bed, a Captain Marvel comic book clutched in his small chubby hand, and smiled serenely up at her.

"I'm afraid this is one of my bad days, Aunt Erin! The ball fell out of my hand and dropped in there again." He pointed toward the sound of dribbling water, his round brown eyes peeping earnestly back at her from behind the large black horn-rim glasses.

With a mute appeal to heaven for self-control, Erin glowered at him and said in a strident voice, "Are you *sure* it slipped, Huntley, or was it perhaps *thrown* in there again?" Her wide gray eyes pinned him to the bed uncomfortably.

"Nope! It slipped, I'm sure." His eyes dropped self-consciously back to his comic book, trying to ignore her penetrating gaze.

"You know, if you were my little boy, I'm afraid I'd have to paddle you for telling stories," Erin told him ominously as she walked past his bed and on into the bathroom. She flinched as her feet sloshed through the deepening puddle of water on the carpeted floor. The one failing that Brenda and Nathan Daniels had, in her opinion, was that they had not disciplined the twins in any way. Brenda had always been a softhearted person, the mere thought of violence sending her into a tizzy. Nathan, on the other hand, had started out to be firm with the children, but it would upset Brenda to the point of hysteria if he threatened to take action with either of them, so he had stopped putting forth the effort. The result sat in the middle of the bed, calmly chewing on a wad of bubble gum that would choke a horse, while his twin came to stand in the doorway to mouth a silent but gleeful "I told you so" to her brother.

Erin stared at the overflowing commode bitterly. It was definitely in need of a plumber again. She sighed as she reached for towels to mop up some of the water. Between their vacation and the plumbing bills, Brenda and Nathan would have to eat hamburger for the rest of the year!

"You spit that gum out of your mouth, Huntley, and

help Holly pick up all the toys you have flung about the living room. As soon as I get this cleaned up and the plumber called"—Erin turned to peep through the bathroom door pointedly at the small boy—*"again,"* she emphasized, "then we are going to eat dinner. And Huntley, it seems I didn't make myself clear this morning . . . If you throw that ball down this toilet *one more time,* I personally will grant you no mercy. You will be spanked and put to bed without your dinner. Is that perfectly clear?"

Solemn dark eyes gaped back up at her, the dire warning finding fertile ground. "I won't, Aunt Erin," he promised earnestly.

As she got down on her hands and knees to sop the water up, Erin heard the twins scurrying out of the room to head for safer ground. It wasn't that they were not totally adorable children, because they most assuredly were. It was hard not to pick them up and hug them a hundred times a day when they were not misbehaving. Holly was the least trouble of the two, a perfect lady most times, usually mortified by her brother's actions, but at other times she had been known to be the ringleader of some of their capers, standing back and looking smug when Huntley was chastised for them. Erin stood up to wring the heavy towel out in the sink. Her eyes were drawn to the reflection in the mirror, and she stared back at Erin Cecile Holmes. No ravishing, sumptuous face stared back at her. No slender, willowy curves met her eyes . . . just a very ordinary twenty-five-year-old face. She studied her soft, naturally curly brown hair, which was styled in a casual pixie cut. Her eyes were a deep pearl gray, and she had a slightly tilted perky nose with just a light smattering of freckles that popped out when she had been in the sun too long, giving her the appearance of a fresh, healthy girl-next-door type. Her mouth was neither too full nor too thin. It was just a normal mouth, or so she thought. Actually Erin was a very attractive woman, but she had convinced herself long ago that she had to work harder than most women to come across as such. All her life she had wished that she had the slim figure and lovely features of her best friend, Brenda, but instead she contented herself with the fact that she had a better personality. By the time they were in their senior year of school, the boys flocked to Brenda in droves, while Erin hung back. The boys always came to cry on her shoulder when Brenda threw them over for a new and more exciting candidate. Erin had always had a heart of pure gold, taking them under her wing, boosting their egos back to the pre-Brenda era and sending them on their way out into the cold cruel world in search of true romance once again. She had never resented her role in life—that is, not until Quinn Adams had entered the scene.

Quinn was a lot older than Brenda and Erin. His smooth, suave good looks made Erin stand in the background and dream young-girlish dreams of what it would be like to catch the eye of such a sophisticated and worldly man. Of course, she never really believed that someone like Quinn would ever look at her twice. And she was right; he didn't. Not at first. His deep, smoldering gaze fell on Brenda, and from then on they dated steadily for several months. If Erin was at Brenda's house when Quinn came to pick Brenda up for a date, Erin would stare out Brenda's window and watch the happy couple walk to the shiny new red convertible and get in, laughing together about some private joke. They would speed away happily into the night, with Brenda molded to Quinn's tall form. Erin would watch them disappear before turning away from the window despondently. It wasn't that she didn't wish Brenda all the happiness in the world; it was simply that she wished that it could be her beside Quinn just once!

Erin sighed as she gathered the wet towels and dropped them in the hamper, then started back to the kitchen. She reached up to touch her forehead, her face feeling hot and flushed. She could hear the petty squabbling of the twins as they worked diligently at restoring order to the family room, with Holly reminding Huntley that he had done the majority of the damage. After checking on the meat loaf she had put in the oven shortly before the last interruption and being satisfied that it was coming along nicely, she made the second call of the day to the plumber, then resumed peeling the potatoes. Against her will, her mind drifted back to the year she was nineteen . . . the year Brenda had married Nathan.

Brenda had graduated the year before her, and she and Quinn still continued to see each other regularly until one day Quinn's older brother, Nathan, who had just been discharged from the service, came home. Both brothers had the same handsome features and were over six feet tall, with wavy dark brown hair, their skin a dark golden bronze, but Nathan's eyes were blue, and Quinn's eyes were a light shade of green. Suddenly it was Nathan who stood on the doorstep to claim Brenda every night. As he would reach out to take her hand, their eyes would meet and the glow that surrounded Brenda seemed to light up the room. Although Nathan was indeed quite handsome, Erin couldn't believe Brenda would throw Quinn over for him.

Erin used to lie in bed at night and dream of what it would be like to be kissed by Quinn. Her young, inquisitive body would shiver in eager anticipation as she imagined him sweeping her into his arms and declaring his love for her. In her dreams she would coolly spurn his ardent advances until he was driven almost mad from wanting her. Finally, in a humane gesture of undeniable goodness, she would relent and ease his agony. It would be late when she finally dozed off, holding her pillow tight against her as she imagined Quinn lying in her arms, sated, happy and hers. Foolish, childish dreams.

Nathan and Brenda's wedding day had not only

changed their lives, it had also changed Erin's. In one short day she went from being an innocent, dreaming girl to a disheartened, frightened woman. Her foolish dream had come true. She had lain in Quinn's arms, and it was all—and more—that she had ever hoped for.

The sound of the cat's high-pitched scream made the paring knife slip from her hands as she whirled and ran into the family room. Huntley was holding a screeching, pawing, spitting cat upside down by the tail while he stood in the middle of the coffee table, his face a stern, determined mask. The cat flailed the air in panic as he hung over the bowl that housed the two goldfish swimming around lazily in the still waters.

"*Huntley Daniels!* Drop that cat instantly!" Erin bellowed, bounding down the two steps that led into the comfortable family room, her nerves stretched taut from the petrified wails coming from the furry feline.

The cat landed hastily with a thump on the table. Springing shakily to his feet, he ran for cover, his yellow body barely a blurred streak as he bolted past a harried Erin.

"He was trying to eat Buck Rogers," Huntley defended swiftly, jumping down off the table nimbly. He ran over to peer intently at the two fish in the bowl. "If he'd eat Cinderella, I wouldn't care, but he was after Buck!" he added heatedly.

"I wouldn't let him eat Cindewella!" Holly shrieked, coming over to give him a sound push. "That dumb old cat's not supposed to be in the house anyway. I'm going to tell Mama when she gets back," she vowed passionately. Her brown eyes were indignant at the prospect of the cat's choice of dinner.

"Both of you just hush!" Erin walked over and took them firmly in hand. "Now why don't you just watch cartoons until I finish making dinner. Then I'll play a game with you," she promised desperately. Anything to restore some peace and quiet. "Do *not* let the cat in again" —she looked at Huntley—"or the dog, or your pet rabbit. Got it?"

"When's Mommy and Daddy coming back?" He wasn't very discreet about whose authority he preferred.

"Not for a while," Erin told him glumly as she switched the TV set on to a loud cartoon. "Dinner will be ready in thirty minutes. See if you can sit here and stay out of trouble that long."

The twins settled back on their bean-bag seats and dismissed her with an impatient glare. If it wasn't for the color of their eyes, Erin would swear she was confronting their uncle Quinn. She had seen the same angry expression on his face when she had done something to displease him. She turned back to the twice-delayed dinner with a heavy heart. That had always been one of the big problems between her and Quinn. She had always upset him when she never meant to. After Brenda and Nathan had announced their engagement, he had started coming around to see her. Erin was never exactly sure why, but she had just assumed she was needed in the crying-shoulder category once again. Although Quinn had never said so, she knew deep down that he was resentful that Brenda had chosen his brother over him. Erin, with her soft heart, tried to make it up to him, building his ego, encouraging him to find someone new. At times it seemed to irritate rather than soothe him when Erin would try her "mother" routine. Although she constantly reminded herself that Quinn would never be seriously attracted to her, she still couldn't keep herself from hoping . . . hoping that someday *she* would be the one beside him. But when reality returned, Erin knew that somewhere in the not-too-distant future another ravishing beauty would capture his attention and that would be the end of her. Quinn Daniels would never be interested in a plain, uninteresting, twenty-pounds-overweight Erin Holmes. She was a lot of things to a lot of people, but she was definitely no dummy!

She smiled grimly to herself as she opened a package of broccoli and put it into the microwave oven. Well, almost no dummy, she thought. Any young girl with stars in her eyes could have made the same mistake she had. It had been six years ago when she had first met him. Erin bit her lower lip as she set the timer and closed the door.

The night she finally succumbed to Quinn's amorous advances had been a magical fairy tale evening for Erin. Positive that Quinn had finally seen the light, she was sure marriage to the man of her dreams was now a mere matter of time. Unfortunately, Quinn hadn't seen that night in quite the same manner. He left town the following morning, leaving a bitter and disillusioned Erin in his wake—a young, inexperienced girl who now felt very cheated, very used. She hadn't seen or heard from him again until a little over a year ago, when he had casually breezed back into town and her life. At first she fought her still-overwhelming attraction to him, telling herself over and over that she was ten times the fool for even giving him the time of day after what he had pulled on her so many years ago. But his charm and persistence won out, and slowly she found herself caught up in his alluring web. Once more her life and thoughts revolved around Quinn Daniels. For several months she allowed herself to dream and believe once again that she would one day be his wife and they would have a marriage like Brenda and Nathan's: perfect. That was what she wanted—the perfect marriage.

It didn't take long for Quinn to rob her of all her hopes and dreams. His eyes began to rove, and it wasn't very long before Erin saw the hopelessness of being involved with a man who would never be satisfied with just one woman. For Quinn there would always be an endless succession of women. Nathan and Quinn Daniels were as different as black and white.

18

Six months ago she had made the final break with Quinn, and he had left the country to work with an oil company in Saudi Arabia. Erin refused to let herself become bitter and disillusioned. Somewhere in this big wide world was the perfect man to fit her idea of the perfect marriage. All she had to do was find him. It certainly would not be a man even remotely similar to Quinn Daniels. She made herself a sacred promise—if she should meet a man six feet tall, she would turn her head in another direction and search for one around five feet eight. If he had green eyes, she would cross the street and look for one who had blue. Should he be unfortunate enough to have a dark complexion, she would walk two miles to find one who was fair-skinned and got sunburned at the drop of a hat. Her perfect man would be the complete opposite of Quinn. That much she had fervently promised her broken heart, and she fully intended to keep that promise.

Erin filled three glasses of milk, then went over to switch off the burners on the stove. Considering what she had gone through in the last few years, she had managed to make a fairly nice life for herself. After Quinn left town the first time, she had gone on to college, then nurse's training, graduating at the head of her class. The problem between her and Quinn had, thankfully, not interfered with her and Brenda's friendship. Brenda had been largely responsible for helping her secure her present position as head nurse of pediatrics at a large medical complex where Brenda used to work in Springfield, Missouri, some fifty miles from where Brenda and Nathan lived, after she had made her final break from Quinn six months earlier.

The blaring sound of the TV caused her to abandon her melancholy thoughts and brought her back to a happier time in her life. Brenda had called unexpectedly one day to plead with her to take some time off to stay with the twins while she and Nathan went away for a while. She

19

had agreed readily, realizing how little time she had spent with her best friend's children. She knew she was letting herself in for trouble with the two unruly five-year-olds, but she figured she could stand anything for a week. One week! It seemed she had been with them a month already, and Brenda had just left yesterday!

The sound of another brush war reached her ears as she hurriedly spooned the potatoes, meat loaf and broccoli onto the plates.

"Red Rover, Red Rover, send Holly and Huntley right over!" Erin yelled into the midst of the miniwar. "Time to eat."

The thundering sound of four feet trying to outrace each other assaulted her in the kitchen as she placed the dinner plates on the table. Another five minutes were lost when she had to escort them back down the hall to the bathroom to wash grubby hands and faces. They finally sat down to a slightly cool dinner, the twins looking at the fare before them suspiciously.

"What's that green stuff?" Huntley asked cautiously, his ever-alert eyes falling on the broccoli.

"Try it, you'll really like it," Erin encouraged, taking a bite of her potatoes and trying to swallow them. I hope I'm not going to have another one of those horrible migraines, she thought despairingly. "See how nicely Holly's eating hers?"

Holly was daintily picking at her plate, her nose turned up sharply as she tasted the green vegetable lying next to her meat.

Huntley stared at his plate, then guardedly brought his fork down slowly to spear a piece of the broccoli. "Ohhhh . . . *YUK!*" He spit out the vegetable nastily, part of it landing next to Holly's plate. "That's sick!"

"*Huntwey!*" his sister screeched loudly, reaching over to pinch him hard on the arm. "Wook what you've done! You are simpwy out of contwol!"

"That stuff's *awful!*" he yelled back at her hotly, his arm knocking over her glass of milk.

Holly reached over and grabbed a handful of his hair as the white liquid dripped down through the cracks of the kitchen table onto the floor. A full-scale assault developed as Erin waded into the middle of the scratching, spitting, biting melee, trying to separate the warring factions. Her head began to throb harder as Huntley's glass of milk tipped over also, spilling into his plate of food.

"Stop it this minute!" Erin yelled over the screaming duo. The twins ignored her totally, each one of them trying to get in the last hit or pinch. Although she worked with children every day, she had *never* come up against such unruly ones!

The family dog started barking from its quarters in the utility room, and the house sounded like feeding time at the zoo, with the dog trying to leap over the wooden barrier that confined him. Erin was trying her best to separate the squealing, fighting twins as Huntley thrust one chubby hand into his plate, grabbed a handful of his mashed potatoes and flung it rudely at Erin. The potato missile hit her squarely in the face, and she gasped in astonishment.

"Huntley Daniels!" she sputtered wildly, wiping at the gooey, pasty mess on her face. "I've warned—" Erin's head jerked up. Through the din, she heard a man's amused voice asking loudly, "Do I need to call the riot squad, or is this just a friendly squabble?"

At the sound of his voice, the room suddenly turned deathly still. Erin could feel the blood drain out of her face as she stood in the ruins of what had once been their dinner. Nearly every dish on the table was overturned, milk was lying in deep puddles on the kitchen floor, and mashed potatoes dripped off her face, landing in wet plops on her white tennis shoes. Taking a deep breath, she smiled up sickly into the amused face of a tall, handsome man.

"Where did you come from?" she whimpered weakly. His presence unnerved her even more. All she needed was a mugger to complete her day! She gazed back at his tall, heavily muscled frame leaning innocently against the doorjamb as he looked at the war-torn kitchen. His brown hair lay in rich, dark waves along the curve of his head, slightly longer than the present trend. A pair of strangely exciting eyes the color of budding leaves after a spring rain was coolly running over her soft curves. They lingered just a little too long on the swell of her breasts, their fullness obviously drawing his attention to the tight T shirt she was wearing.

When he finally spoke, his voice was deep, like rich, soft velvet, his eyes still lingering on her. "I rang the doorbell, but apparently you didn't hear it. I took the liberty of coming on in. It was obvious someone was home . . ." he added dryly, fighting to overcome the overwhelming desire to laugh out loud at her flustered countenance.

"You should have waited until I answered the door!" she snapped, suddenly coming out of her shock at seeing him standing there. She reached up hurriedly and tried to wipe more of the potatoes off her face discreetly.

"Let's see, I believe the name is—Erin, am I right?" he said, undaunted by her cool greeting.

"Yes, you're right," she answered coolly, her hands trying to straighten up some of the disorder before her. His face seemed to ring a bell in her memory, but she was powerless to come up with a name.

The twins had ceased their brawling and tumbled out of their chairs exuberantly to throw their arms around the man's legs and squeeze them tightly.

"Uncle Price, Uncle Price," they both chorused. "Did you bring us a surprise?"

Price looked down at the chattering monkeys wrapped

around his legs and grinned skeptically. "Do you think you deserve anything?"

"Yeah, yeah, we've been *good*!" they vowed seriously as they excitedly bounced up and down.

Erin glared at them in disbelief. If this man believed that, he was crazy! "Yes, I can see just how good you've been," he agreed calmly.

The twins ceased their jumping, their brown eyes guiltily surveying the demolished table and their aunt with potatoes still clinging to her face.

"It was *his* fault," Holly returned promptly, pointing her finger at Huntley accusingly. "Don't give him his present, Uncle Price," she urged, sticking her thumb in her mouth to suck on it. "He's been vewy unwuly all day," she advised between sucks.

"Take your thumb out of your mouth," Erin said as she swiped the traces of potato lingering in white, flaking patches. Her mind was in a chaotic state as she took Holly's thumb out of her mouth and wiped at the milk running down the front of her blouse. Price . . . oh, yes . . . Nathan's best man had been named Price.

"I'll tell you what I'll do," Price bargained, reaching over to set the two milk glasses upright again. "You and your brother sit back down at the table and finish your dinner—quietly," he stressed with a stern look at both of them. "Then we'll go looking for surprises. Deal?"

"Deal, deal!" they shouted excitedly, scrambling for their deserted chairs once again.

Price helped the twins back into their seats as Erin went to the cabinet for two more clean plates and glasses. In a matter of minutes sanity had been restored, and the twins were obediently and placidly eating their meal.

Price looked up from his place beside Holly, his emerald gaze capturing Erin's. "Okay, guys, now you finish eating quietly. I'd like to talk to Erin in the other room for a minute, if that's all right with her." He smiled pleasantly.

Erin's pulse leaped for a moment at the sound of his deep voice. It reminded her painfully of another man's voice . . . She nervously brushed her hands down the sides of her jeans, wondering what he would want to talk to her about.

"We will!" the twins agreed angelically, spooning their broccoli into their mouths eagerly.

Price steered Erin into the family room, sidestepping the mounds of toys scattered haphazardly around the room.

"Those children," Erin muttered helplessly as she rescued a doll from beneath Price's faltering steps. "I thought they had cleaned up this mess!"

Price laughed. "They probably did, but if I remember correctly, they can tear up a steel ball bearing in the time it takes to blink an eye."

Erin grinned back at him. "You remember very correctly."

Price extended a friendly hand toward Erin. "The name's Price Seaver. And although I do remember your first name, I'm afraid that for the life of me, I can't recall the last." He smiled in apology.

"Holmes." Erin's head began to throb painfully once more, her stomach growing queasier by the moment. Her eyes fastened on the man standing before her, and though she was totally unaware that she was gaping, that was exactly what she was doing. To her knowledge, she had seen Price Seaver only once in her life—the night of Brenda and Nathan's marriage—but for some uncanny reason he reminded her of Quinn. She mentally shook herself as she tried to concentrate on what Price was saying to her. Something about being in town and wanting to stop for a minute to visit with Nathan. The way his dark brown, wavy hair lay on his shirt collar in a careless yet very controlled manner—the unusual shade of sparkling green eyes—the thick dark lashes making them look lazy and cool—the way he towered above her medium height when he spoke to her—was she becoming paranoid?

"Erin." Price stopped in mid-sentence and looked at her self-consciously. "Am *I* the one with mashed potatoes on my face?"

"What? Uh . . . no . . . No, I'm sorry. Look, would you mind if I got a washcloth to wipe this stickiness off my face?" Erin's face blushed a deep pink as she realized she had literally been gawking at the poor man! She left the living room and returned quickly holding the wet cloth against her face.

"What did you want to see me about?" she demanded curtly.

Price looked a bit startled at her abrupt change of mood, but he recovered quickly. "Nothing, really. I just thought we'd give those two little hoodlums time to eat their dinner alone. Are you baby-sitting for the evening?"

Erin's hand went to her temple, and she massaged the throbbing area urgently. Her head felt as though it were going to burst anytime now.

"Brenda and Nathan have gone on a short vacation. I'm staying with the children until they get back."

Price let out a low whistle, his eyes watching her fingers knead her temples in concerned detachment. "You must be some kind of friend to take on a job like that," he observed with admiration.

Erin managed a weak smile at the sound of reverence in his voice. "I must admit that I had forgotten how—active the twins are."

"Active! They're like a double charge of dynamite going off every hour on the hour." Price grinned, his white teeth flashing attractively in his bronze face.

Erin groaned and buried her face in her hands. Everything about this Price Seaver reeked of Quinn Daniels!

"Is there something wrong with you?" Price asked, his voice filled with concern now.

"No, I'm just tired and I have a headache, Mr. Seaver. If you'd like, I'll tell Brenda and Nathan you stopped by. They'll be back in about a week; maybe you can come back then," Erin told him as she rose to her feet and started ushering him to the door. What she wanted most right now was to get this painful reminder of Quinn out of the house, the twins in their beds, and to collapse in her own.

"Why do I get the distinct impression you're trying to get rid of me?" Price grinned as she nearly shoved him toward the front door. Suddenly he stopped and looked at her strangely. "I promised the twins a surprise when they finished their meal, *Ms. Holmes.* Do you mind?"

"Yes, I do mind. Go home."

"I beg your pardon." He cocked a disbelieving eyebrow in her direction.

"I said, go home!" Erin knew she was being unreasonably rude, but for some strange reason she couldn't care less. "Leave the twins' surprise with me and I'll see that they get it."

"Have I done something to offend you, Ms. Holmes?"

"Don't be silly. Of course you haven't offended me." Erin started to push at his reluctant form once more. "It's getting late and I want to put the twins to bed early."

Price glanced at his watch. "At five o'clock!"

"Is it just five? It seems like it's midnight!" Erin groaned.

"Now look, Erin, I don't want to make waves, but after all, I did stop by to see the twins . . ."

"You said you came to see Brenda and Nathan!" Erin said sharply.

"Brenda and Nathan *and* the twins!" He rudely jerked her hand off his arm. "What is your problem, lady?"

"My problem, Mr. Seaver! My problem! If you want me to be completely honest, then I'll just tell you *my* problem!" Erin's temper was boiling and her head felt as if it were being squeezed in a vise, causing her to throw caution and good manners to the wind. "I don't like you, Mr. Seaver!" She opened the front door and literally shoved a bewildered Price out on the front porch.

"Will you just knock off the shoving and tell me what's going on!" Price bellowed impatiently as he was thrown out into the cool late-afternoon air. "What did I do?"

"It's not what you did but what you are. If you want to get technical, I don't like men who are six feet tall, I *detest* men with brown wavy hair, and I particularly resent a man who has your color eyes!" Her own eyes were flashing fire at the moment. "To sum it all up for you, Mr. Seaver, I can't stand the sight of you!" She slammed the door angrily in his stunned face.

No sooner had the door banged shut than a loud pounding began, followed by the persistent peal of the doorbell. Erin leaned against the door, aghast at what had just taken place. Her head hammered sickly as she covered her face with her hands and nearly wept. What in the world had gotten into her? True, Price Seaver bore a faint resemblance to Quinn Daniels, but certainly nothing strong enough to bring on an unreasonable reaction as strong as what she had just experienced.

The banging grew more heated as Erin whirled and jerked the door open furiously. "What is it now?!" she screeched.

"I want to tell the kids good-bye, *if* you don't mind." Price glared at her stormily, then shoved his way past her into the room, mumbling obscenities under his breath. "I wasn't aware when I stopped in here tonight that I was going to be dealing with a psycho—"

"Just say your good-byes and leave, Mr. Seaver. I'm not interested in a clinical diagnosis of my behavior," Erin cut him off sharply.

Price walked toward the kitchen, stopped to turn and look back at Erin. "If I had to take a guess, lady, I'd guess

27

that I remind you of one doozy of a heel," he couldn't resist adding in a nasty tone.

A swift light of pain streaked through the angry gray eyes that met his now. For one brief moment Price felt a surge of unwanted protectiveness toward the pale young woman who stood before him. Somewhere down the line she had obviously been very hurt by a man with Price's characteristics, enough to sour her on *all* men, apparently. Well, it was certainly no concern of his. He had his own problems, and the last thing he was interested in was playing nursemaid to some hot-tempered hellcat who was trying to get over an old lover.

"Well, if you'll excuse me, I hate to leave your stimulating company but I'll just see the kids before I go. Next time I'm in town I'll be sure to look you up . . ." Price's voice was sinking rapidly now as Erin blinked her eyes and stared up blankly at him. "Erin? Is there something wrong with you? Are you ill . . ." Price's temper faded quickly as he moved toward her, trying to elicit some response from her.

"Mr. Seaver . . . excuse me . . . but I'm . . . I think I'm going to be sick . . ."

A swift, terrifying black abyss began to swallow her slowly. Her last coherent thoughts were of strong arms going around her, pulling her close to a broad muscular chest. It was unexpected; it was most assuredly not wanted; but Erin Holmes was once again in the arms of a man who was six feet tall, had dark wavy hair and beautiful green eyes.

CHAPTER TWO

Erin wasn't sure how long she was unconscious, but when she awoke there were four chubby hands gently patting her cheeks. A cool cloth had been laid across her forehead, but the tight, almost unbearable pain was still pulsating in her head.

"You'll be awight, Aunt Erin," Holly assured her, tenderly patting her cheek with a greasy, meat-loaf-smelling hand. "Uncle Pwice is gonna take care of you."

Erin moaned, her stomach turning over at the faint smell of the greasy food. "Thank you, Holly, but I'll be all right." She tried to raise her head but was stopped by a firm hand.

"Just lie still, Erin. You've been out for a few minutes."

Price leaned down, the vague aroma of a very sexy aftershave reaching her nose as he carefully wiped her face with the wet cloth.

"Please . . . Price . . ." She reached to halt his hand. "I'll be fine. Thank you."

His touch sent tiny shivers rocketing through her, only adding to her pain. "That may be so, but you're going to lie there for a while anyway. What caused you to black out?" he asked, draping a light afghan around her legs gently.

"I have migraine headaches occasionally. I've felt one coming on all day," she said wearily, closing her eyes against the pain.

29

"Migraines? Those can be pretty rough," Price said softly.

"I was in a car accident several years ago, and I've had them ever since."

"Do you have any medicine with you?" he asked, pulling the twins off her. "Why don't you guys go find something to do in your room," he suggested firmly, steering them in the direction of their bedroom.

"Can we watercolor?" Huntley asked hopefully. One could practically see the wheels turning in his head.

"Sure, sure . . . Just keep the noise down, okay, pal? Your aunt Erin's not feeling well," he agreed absently.

Erin was in so much pain she was barely aware of the conversation going on around her. She was fighting hard not to disgrace herself and regurgitate on the living room floor.

"Oh boy!" Huntley made a beeline for his room, with Holly following in hot pursuit. The loud slam of their bedroom door shook the house as they gleefully searched for their paints and brushes.

"Look, why don't I carry you into your bed. This couch doesn't look very comfortable to me," Price suggested, kneeling next to her. He was being so kind, it made her hurt even more.

"Oh, Price, just go away," she moaned, fighting her nausea and losing.

"I'd like nothing better!" he snapped tensely. Gone was the tender tone that had been in his voice earlier. "But I hardly think you're in any condition to be here by yourself."

"I'll be fine . . . just give me a minute," she whimpered.

"How long are Brenda and Nathan going to be gone, did you say?"

"They won't be home for a week." Just go away, Price, she wanted to scream. This day had been a total nightmare for her.

30

Price stood up and began to pace the floor, rubbing the back of his neck with one large hand. "A week! How in the devil did you consent to watch those—holy terrors for a week? I can't stand to be around them one hour, let alone one week!"

A small smile flickered across Erin's face as she lay with her eyes closed. She could well imagine those twins in his care for a week. He seemed to be immaculate in his dress, and his life was probably well organized. Children would no doubt interfere very much in Price Seaver's way of life.

"I don't get to see them very often," she murmured. "I wanted to spend some time with them, so I agreed when Brenda asked me."

"You'll be sorry," he predicted grimly, increasing his pacing. "They'll have you pulling your hair out by the roots in a week."

Ha! A week, she thought dryly. How about one day!

"I love the little rascals," he hastened to add, "but that darn Nathan lets them get away with murder. They set fire to my briefcase last time I was here. Burned every damn paper in it," he reminisced incredulously, shaking his head as if he still couldn't believe it. "If they were mine, I'd take some of that out of them but quick!" he promised.

"I know," Erin commiserated, "but it certainly isn't my place to clamp down on them."

Price stopped his pacing and walked back over to peer down at her grayish green face intently. "How long do these headaches last?"

"Days," she admitted bleakly, wishing she could self-destruct.

"Well . . . darn it! You can't take care of those kids in your condition," he said.

"I'll have to."

"You couldn't if you tried," he observed. "I suppose I'll have to find someone to come and give you a hand . . ." He sounded put out at this shoddy turn of fate.

Erin's eyes flew open, her stomach churning violently. "You certainly will not!" Brother, that's all she would need to top her day off. Have him running around doing her favors! "I can manage—somehow," she said grimly.

"Listen, you—twerp! Someone's got to assume control here! You can't even lift your head off the pillow," he said, "let alone corral two walking time bombs!"

"I was doing fine till you came on the scene," she answered angrily, fighting her way out of the entanglement of the afghan. When she stood up, bright lights danced in front of her eyes, and she wanted to cry with humiliation as the long overdue heaves assaulted her.

Price was at her side instantly, sweeping her up in his strong arms. He made a mad dash down the hall as Erin fought to hold on until they reached the bathroom. He laid her down near the toilet, holding her head for her as she emptied her stomach over and over, disgracing herself miserably. Tears blinded her as she tried to push Price back, so embarrassed she wanted to die. But he firmly yet tenderly held her head for her, patting her comfortingly until the violent heaving subsided. Leaving for a moment, he wet another washcloth and came back to her to lay it gently on her clammy brow, wiping her flushed face. He spoke soothing words to her as she slumped weakly against his broad chest. "Take it easy, Erin. Just lie back and relax."

"Price . . . Please, you don't have to stay in here," she protested sickly.

"I know I don't," he replied softly, smoothing back the wet locks of her curly brown hair, "but I want to. Are you any better?" he asked after a moment, wrapping her warmly in his arms to still the explosive trembling of her body.

"I think so. Can you help me to my room?" She was beyond fighting now. She just wanted to bury herself in a hole and never come out.

"I think I can handle that." He swooped her up in his arms effortlessly and carried her back into the hall. "Which room?" he asked, looking down into her face. Erin's breath caught at the radiance of his smile.

"The first one on the right," she told him. Her heart skipped a beat—two beats—as he pressed her tightly against his chest and turned toward her bedroom. She was extremely conscious of the extra ten pounds she was carrying and mentally flayed herself for eating that extra doughnut for breakfast this morning. "You don't have to carry me," she protested. "I know I'm too heavy. I've been meaning to go on a diet," she finished lamely as he strode down the hall with her easily.

"You're not heavy," he reproached mildly.

"Yes, yes I am," she insisted, feeling like a fool. "I should take off ten pounds at least!" Her face flamed when she thought of what he must be thinking. Men did not like to carry a butterball in their arms!

"I could stand to lose a few pounds myself," he grunted as they entered her bedroom and he laid her down on the bed.

Erin stared up at his lean, trim frame and wondered where he could possibly afford to lose an ounce. He was all muscle, all virile man, and she resented it with every ounce of flab on her!

"You're just being nice," she muttered as she lay back against the pillow weakly. "I know I'm fat and—plain!"

"All right," he agreed readily, "you're a tub of lard and your face would stop a clock. Now, if that makes you feel better, maybe you'll be in the mood to tell me if you have any medicine with you."

Erin's face clouded over. He certainly didn't have to be so brutally frank. "In my purse on the vanity," she said tightly.

Price rummaged through her purse, coming up with a

brown plastic vial. "These?" He held up the bottle questioningly.

"Yes," she muttered.

"Stay right where you are, troll. I'll get you some water to take these with." Price stepped into the small bath off her room.

"I can do without the insults," she said huffily, untying her tennis shoes and kicking them to the floor miserably.

"Whatever you say," he said blandly as he returned with a glass of water and two pills. "Is this how you get your kicks? Running yourself down?"

"I'm not running myself down," she replied. "I just don't try to fool myself. I know that I'm not the raving beauty Brenda is. . . ." Her voice trailed off as she avoided his gaze, embarrassed.

He stood beside the bed staring down at her intently, his assessing eyes revealing nothing. The silence lengthened as she brought the pills to her trembling mouth and swallowed them with a small sip of water. Their eyes met again as she handed the glass back to him and lay back on her pillow.

"Feel better now?" he inquired gently.

"Not really," she said and groaned.

"Well, we need to figure out what we're going to do. I should be going soon."

"Nobody's making you stay," Erin said. "You're free to go anytime."

Price ignored her words as he walked over to gaze out the window paneled with sea-foam-green drapes. The view was breathtaking from where he stood looking out into the gathering dusk. The majestic A frame that Nathan and Brenda had built nestled in a bluff overlooking Table Rock Lake. The rising moon was glistening on the tranquil waters. A warm breeze trickled through the open window.

"I wonder if there's a neighbor who could come in and help with the children tonight," he mused. "It appears you're hard pressed to control the children even when you're well, let alone now."

She knew he was recalling the scene he had walked in on earlier. "Price," Erin said as she raised herself up on one elbow, giving him a withering glare, "if there's one thing I don't need right now, it's you telling me my faults. Now you know where the door is—please use it!"

"Get off my back, Erin. I'm stuck here for the night and you know it." He turned away from the window, his face a stony mask. "If those pills are what I think they are, you're going to be out like a light any second now."

Erin moaned. She had forgotten how powerful the medicine was. Sometimes she slept for hours after taking the pills.

"I haven't checked into a motel yet, so I'll just use Nathan and Brenda's bedroom for the night. Tomorrow I'll try to find someone to come and stay with the children until you get on your feet again."

Loud, shrilling war whoops pierced the night. The sound of running feet assaulted their ears as the bedroom door flew open and Huntley and Holly stormed in, riding their imaginary war ponies.

"Oh, good lord!" Price said with a groan, surveying the rainbow-colored faces and paint-stained clothes of the two standing before him. "What have you done to your-selves?"

"We're Indians, Uncle Price," Huntley said, letting out another loud war cry. "This is my squaw, Horseface," he said, jerking a smeared thumb at his sister. "I painted her all up!"

"Huntwey! I do not want to be Horseface! I want to be Wunning Water," Holly screeched indignantly, reaching over and thumping him smartly on his feather.

Huntley reached back and jerked her tomahawk out of her hand and swung at her wildly. "*I'm* chief and *I* give the orders, squaw!" he railed hotly.

Price stepped between them, his tall presence casting a blight over the arrogant chief's authority. "*I* happen to be the chief around here, and I'm ordering you to stop this fighting!" he told them harshly, trying to dodge the flying watercolor-painted hands that were destroying his spotless buff-color trousers. "When I told you you could watercolor, I thought you meant in your coloring books! Why in the devil did you paint yourselves up like that? Just look at this mess," he fumed, holding Holly's face between two strong fingers.

Streaks of red, blue, gold and purple were drawn all over her pretty little features, with two big round black circles drawn around each eye. "She looks like a crazed raccoon," he observed disgustedly.

Huntley leaned over and peered at his sister intently. "Yow, she does kinda, doesn't she?" he agreed in awe.

Holly set up a penetrating wail that tore through Erin's head like a buzz saw. "I don't want to look like a waccoon," she cried pitifully. "Huntwey said I could be a squaw!"

Erin covered her ears in pain. "Oh, Holly, please . . ."

"All right, you two." Price started ushering the twins out of the bedroom forcefully. "We're going to let your aunt Erin sleep now. Let's go get you cleaned up." He surveyed their condition once again. "What a mess!"

The children quieted instantly as Price led them out of the room and marched them down the hall. Erin was beginning to feel the merciful effects of the medicine taking hold as she slid down onto her pillow. She was just floating into an inky void when she dimly heard Price's astonished voice as he apparently reached the twins' bedroom.

"Good lord! What have you done to your room!"

The rest of the night was a total blank to Erin. The pills sent her into a deep, painless sleep. When she awoke the

36

next morning to the chatter of the twins playing in their room, she was surprised to find the sun barely peeking over a hill. Her head still throbbed, and her mouth felt like cotton. Glancing at the clock near her bed, she noticed it was barely six o'clock. The twins were not noted for "sleeping in." She sat up hesitantly on the side of the bed; the room whirled for a minute. With all the strength she could muster, she stood and made her way slowly into the small bath. Ten minutes later she had washed her face and brushed her teeth but still felt like someone was using a jackhammer in her head. She stepped out into the hall and walked cautiously to the door of the twins' room. The medicine had made her feel shaky and weak. "Good morning, children." She smiled softly. "Where's your uncle Price?"

"Still sweeping," Holly said irritably, her tone suggesting that it was hard to believe anyone would still be in bed at this hour.

"I'm hungry, Aunt Erin," Huntley said, his brown eyes peeping hopefully up at her from behind his large glasses. "Can we eat now?"

Erin sagged weakly against the door frame, her head begging for more medicine. "I don't know if I can fix you anything right now, Huntley. Could you wait until Price gets up?" she asked hopefully.

"Could we wake him up?" Huntley asked expectantly. "Mommy and Daddy let us wake them up when we're hungry—and we're *awful* hungry," he added for insurance.

"Well . . . I don't know. . . ."

"Oh, goody, goody, we can!" Huntley grabbed for Holly's hand. "Let's go, Holly. Maybe he'll fix us pancakes," he schemed as he bolted past Erin, heading across the hall.

"Huntley! Wait a minute," Erin said, trying to catch up with the flying feet. The twins burst into Price's room, the door slamming back against the wall, the sound reverberating around the room like an explosion. Price's head came off his pillow instantly and he looked around in confusion as the twins landed in the middle of his bed exuberantly.

"What—what's going on?" he asked, befuddled, trying to control their hugs.

"We're hungry, Uncle Price. Aunt Erin said you would fix us some pancakes!" Huntley said pitifully, getting up close to Price's face. His small hand came out to explore the heavy stubble on his uncle's face.

Erin gasped as she stood in the doorway. "Now *wait* a minute, Huntley. I did *not* say that he would fix you pancakes!" Erin had to smother a grin at the look of complete bafflement covering Price's sleepy face. Her pulse raced as he sat up and ran his fingers through his thick, tousled hair. His broad, muscular chest was covered with thick, dark brown hair that ran enticingly all the way down to where the sheet fell below his waist.

Price glanced up, seeing her in the doorway as the twins continued their early-morning chatter, filling him in on what they wanted with the pancakes.

"Okay, okay! Just pipe down for a minute," he said, gently hugging them to his chest, then glancing back at Erin's pale face. "You all right this morning?"

Erin gave him a shaky smile. "Not really. I'm afraid I'm going to have to take some more medicine . . . I'm sorry," she murmured at the bleak look that returned to his face.

Holly jumped off the bed and crossed the room to take Erin's hand in her small one. "Come on, Aunt Ewin, we all have to kiss each other good morning," she proclaimed firmly, leading her over to Price's bed.

"What?" Erin laughed questioningly as Holly pushed her down on the bed, then hopped back up to her place beside Huntley and Price. "Evewyone has to kiss each other good morning. That's what Mommy and Daddy

38

do," she said earnestly, leaning over to kiss Price on the mouth soundly.

A frantic round of kisses was exchanged between the twins and their aunt and uncle. Erin had to laugh at their enthusiasm as they wrapped their arms around Price's neck and squeezed him tight, nearly knocking him over in the bed.

"Now you and Uncle Pwice kiss good morning," Holly instructed sweetly.

The smiles dropped from Price's and Erin's faces immediately. Erin flushed a bright red as Huntley and Holly waited for the morning ritual to be completed.

"I—don't think that's necessary," Erin hedged, lowering her eyes in embarrassment.

"But Mommy and Daddy always do," Holly said, her brown eyes puzzled.

Erin hazarded a glance at Price, who was obviously enjoying her discomfort. Holly reached up and brought the two reluctant heads together. "You gotta kiss," she issued huffily, nearly knocking their heads together. Erin's startled gray eyes stared back into Price's slightly amused emerald ones as he said teasingly, "Yeah, you gotta, Aunt Erin!"

Erin leaned forward slightly and pecked Price on the cheek quickly.

"No . . ." Holly groaned morosely. "Not like *that*. Like this!" She reached up and smacked Price hard on the mouth again. "See!" With grim determination she shoved Erin's face back into Price's amused one. "Now *weally* kiss him!" she ordered.

"Yeah, Aunt Erin," Price said as he grinned smugly. "Don't you know how to weally kiss a man good morning?" he taunted, his voice sounding very low and sexy.

Erin felt a strange weakness invade her as Price leaned closer and touched his mouth to hers lightly. Her eyes dropped shut as she froze for a moment, savoring the feel of his mouth on hers. His lips brushed hers gently once again, silently urging a response. She opened her eyes slowly to meet his, and with a sigh of defeat she hesitantly brought her lips to touch tremblingly against his more firmly. Price's hands reached out to clasp the back of her curly head, drawing her closer into his arms, his mouth closing over hers.

The months melted away, and suddenly Erin was back in Quinn's arms with his mouth devouring hers in searing, demanding intensity. They both seemed to forget their surroundings and the two sets of dark brown eyes that watched them, bored, as Price held her captive in his seductive embrace.

She heard him moan softly as he reluctantly broke the kiss, his hands tightening painfully around her throbbing head. It had been a long time since he had kissed a woman this way and, surprisingly, it felt good.

Impatient hands broke them apart as Erin looked into Price's lazy, slumbrous eyes, eyes that told her that if they were alone, he might ask for more than a kiss from her. "That's enough!" Huntley proclaimed. "You've got it right. That's how Mommy and Daddy do it."

Price wouldn't release her eyes from his burning gaze as he answered softly, "You're sure? I want to be sure it's *exactly* as your parents do it."

"It is!" Holly affirmed, jumping off the bed. " 'Cept sometimes Daddy wants us to go back and play in our room for a little while. He says if we're *weal* quiet and don't bother him and Mommy, he'll fix us something weeealllly special for bweakfast," she said in childlike innocence.

"I'll just bet he does," Price said, his gaze still locked with Erin's. "I wonder if that would work for me," he murmured low.

Erin snapped out of her stupor and drew back guiltily from his arms. "Don't be ridiculous. I don't plan on making *that* mistake but once in my life," she said curtly as the twins scampered out of the room, heading for the kitchen. She had not mistaken the innuendo in his veiled comment.

Price stretched like a lazy panther lying in the sun, his muscles flexing taut in the early-morning light. The sheet slipped precariously low over his hips. "Why, my dear Erin, are you saying the heel I look like took unfair advantage of you at one time?" His cool green gaze pinned her to the floor as he continued in a low, clipped tone. "You don't need to worry. A woman is the last thing I want in my life at the present, no matter how casual the encounter." His voice was very cold and indifferent now.

Erin's eyes turned as cool and glacial as his, her patience at an end with his blatant arrogance. "You cocky, pompous, egotistical—jackass! My private life is no concern of yours whatsoever!" Tears blurred her eyes as she started backing out the bedroom door, wanting only to find refuge from this hurtful man and her pounding head.

"But Erin," Price said from his bed, "surely I haven't upset you again! I don't recall making any indecent suggestion to you. You really have a problem with men, don't you? I wonder what would happen to me if I actually *did* make a pass at you." He chuckled wickedly.

"You're disgusting!" She whirled and started out the door, then paused to add briefly, "And you certainly will never find me in your bed! I may not be the raving beauty Brenda is, but I would never lower myself to sleep with a man like you, Price. Don't ever forget that!"

Price looked at her disgustedly. Why did she keep bringing her looks into their conversation! "Don't make rash statements you can't live with," he shouted as she tramped down the hall. "I may be willing to put a brown paper sack over your head and pretend that you're not a homely little—twerp!" he yelled after her as he heard her bedroom door slam. He thought about her for a moment

41

after she left the room, wondering why she seemed so hung up on her looks. He thought she was a living doll! But he wasn't interested.

Erin crawled back under her blankets miserably, cursing the day she had ever met Price Seaver. She groaned, turning over onto her stomach and burying her head deeper into the pillow, trying to block the pain and the anger but failing with both. The thought of getting up to get her medicine was just too much at the moment, so she lay in acute torment. The door to her room slid open quietly, and she heard soft footsteps coming over to her bed. Strong, compassionate arms lifted her, then turned her gently onto her back once more as a cold cloth came to rest on her forehead. The hands that ministered to her were tough, calloused hands, yet they handled her as if she were a fragile possession that would break easily if grasped too hard.

"Take these," Price ordered gruffly, yet his gentle eyes told another story. Erin groped blindly for the pills and swallowed them gratefully while he held her head up off the pillow. After offering her one more sip of water, he carefully let her head slip back down onto the pillow.

"Can't the doctors do anything about these?" he asked softly, rearranging the bedding and tucking it in close around her.

"No. It's possible they may go away someday, but right now I have to learn to live with them." In all her life she had never experienced such tenderness. Somehow, with Price sitting beside her, the pain wasn't as bad as it had been earlier.

"Do you think you can eat something?" he asked, leaning over to wipe her forehead with the cloth. "You didn't have your dinner last night."

Erin's stomach rolled at the thought of food. "No, please . . . I couldn't eat a thing. Just make sure the children are fed."

"They're in there putting their clothes on right now, then I'm going to try to tackle pancakes," he said grimly, removing the cloth and taking it into the bathroom to moisten it again.

The last thing in the world Erin felt like doing was carrying on a conversation, yet she didn't want to end it. It seemed nice to have a man to talk to for a change. She had steered clear of men for so many months now, she had almost forgotten how deep a male voice could sound or how nice it was to be touched by a man's hands.

Price came back out of the bathroom and went to her vanity, pulling open the top drawer and rummaging through it quietly.

"What are you doing?" she asked, startled.

"I'm looking for one of your gowns," he said absently, extracting a sheer blue one. He examined it closely, then, satisfied with his selection, closed the drawer and came back to her. "Can you sit up for a minute?" he asked, his hands pulling her upward.

"Price!" Erin struggled to clear her head as the medicine began to weave its magic. "What do you think you're doing?" she asked groggily.

"Something I should have done last night," he said, avoiding her swatting hands. "Knock it off, Erin! I'm going to get you into something more comfortable."

He threw back the cover, and Erin's face flooded with color as he stripped her jeans off with one slick motion. He had obviously had lots of practice! Then he hooked his thumbs around her bikini panties. "You'll only make your head hurt worse with all that squirming," he warned, undaunted in his task. "I don't see what the problem is. Just pretend I'm a doctor," he told her, stripping her panties just as smoothly, then letting them join her jeans on the floor.

"A doctor!" Erin protested, letting herself be handled like an infant. "No doctor ever stripped me like this!"

"Don't worry. I have bad eyesight," he said with a grin as he pulled her T shirt over her head indifferently. When he unsnapped her bra and her soft breasts fell loose, Price's eyes lingered uncommonly long on their feminine loveliness, his eyes turning darker. "Now I must admit this is a little harder to ignore."

"You are—horrible!" Erin sputtered, her face flaming a bright red. "If I weren't so sick I'd slap your smirking face!" she said crossly, feeling the heat from his gaze on her breasts. The dark centers began to tighten and grow taut under his continuing scrutiny.

"I'm just a disinterested bystander trying to be helpful," he said easily. His eyes dropped back to her face as he reached for her gown, slipping it over her head. "Keep telling yourself that. It'll make it easier."

"Disinterested, my foot!" she replied staunchly, slapping his hand as he brushed it over one breast tauntingly before he stood up.

"You have a nasty disposition, do you realize that?" Price said, laying her back down gently. "If I were in your boots I'd be grateful someone was kind enough to take his valuable time and help me when I needed it."

"I don't need your help," Erin replied irritably, snuggling back down.

A broad grin crossed Price's face. "Now you and I both know that's not true, so why don't you just lie back like a good girl and get over your headache so I can get back to my own life."

Erin looked up at him heatedly. "Don't kid yourself. I do not need you, Price Seaver!"

"Oh, bull! Just go to sleep, Erin. You're a hopeless case!" Price strode to the door and jerked it open. "I'm going to scour this neighborhood for someone to take over before I lose my religion with you!" He slammed the door with a disgusted whack.

Erin cringed as the door shuddered, her eyes closing

painfully at the sound. He was so rude! Her heart thudded when she thought of his parting words, but reason overtook her quickly. She hoped he did find someone!

She squeezed her eyes shut, willing herself to block out his handsome face and the thrill of his earlier kiss. No more foolish dreams, that was a promise. But was it one she could keep?

Unconsciously she balled her fists in angry protest against the unknown forces that were once again cruelly placing her in the path of a man who could cause her anesthetized heart to show some flickering signs of life. She didn't *want* to feel that exhilarating surge of awareness when he touched her. She didn't *want* her foolish heart to beat faster when his gaze nonchalantly met hers or his shoulder accidentally brushed hers as he passed her in a room. And most of all she didn't want to remember just how good it had felt to be in a man's arms, even as innocently as she had been in Price's. She could not fall in love. She would not!

CHAPTER THREE

It was barely seven o'clock when Erin opened her eyes again. She lay very still, listening for the sounds of the children's voices, but she could hear nothing. The house was wreathed in silence. Just for one delicious moment she remembered that Price was somewhere near—or perhaps that was the reason for the silent house. Maybe he had found someone to look after the children while she was sleeping and had left. A stab of fear pierced her heart at that thought. She was just being foolish again. What did it matter whether he was still here? In the end he would leave.

Reaching for the robe that Price must have draped over the foot of the bed, she rose to walk cautiously into the bathroom. Her headache was beginning to show signs of letting up, the tight band of pain releasing its grip gradually. She wet a clean cloth and ran it lightly across her face, groaning audibly as she saw her rumpled reflection in the mirror. What a mess! Her hair was standing on end, her face was pale and sickly, large black circles hung under her eyes. What Price must think of her! She caught her errant thoughts quickly. Why should she care what he thought of her. Still. . . .

In the last few years she had learned to use makeup to her advantage, and her hair was styled in a cut that was most becoming to her face. Yes, although she was still no Brenda, she might impress Price . . . But heavens! Look at her now! And this was how he had seen her from the time he had entered the door—and with the potatoes on her face!

With a disgusted shrug of her shoulders, she laid the cloth back down. If she ever did see Price again, she would make sure she looked her best. He wouldn't be interested, but it would do her ego a world of good after this disastrous meeting.

The dry cotton feeling that still lingered in her mouth even after a vigorous brushing plus mouthwash had to be appeased. On shaky legs she started down the hall in search of something cool to drink. She was distracted by the family room as she passed, taking note of its neat, orderly appearance. Nothing was out of place except— She paused and reversed her steps to walk closer to the coffee table. Kneeling, she peered unbelievingly into the small fishbowl, catching her breath in surprise. Buck Rogers and Cinderella were both floating, stiff as boards, on top of the soapy water. What could have happened, she thought in panic as her eyes searched anxiously for any sight of the twins. She didn't want to think of what their reaction would be when they found their prized pets bobbing on top of the water, cushioned in a mound of soapsuds!

E.T., the family dog, let out a pitiful yelp from his place of confinement, bringing Erin back to a standing position. He undoubtedly wanted his dinner. Price had probably been too busy trying to keep up with the children to worry about trying to feed the Daniels' menagerie. As she neared the kitchen, she heard a murmur of voices from behind the closed door to the utility room. She couldn't help but notice the spotless kitchen, everything gleaming and immaculate—a far cry from when she last saw it! Whoever Price had gotten was certainly efficient—far more so than she had been.

The sight that met her eyes as she quietly pushed open

47

the door to the utility room was one of calm tranquillity. Both twins were sitting next to Price, their faces and clothes sparkling clean, munching contentedly on apples. Their young, inquisitive eyes watched their uncle patiently trying to wipe green enamel off one side of the once-white dog.

They looked up as the door opened, smiling brightly at Erin.

"Hi, Aunt Erin," they greeted her. Price turned his head and surveyed her barely concealed curves as she stood in the doorway, his eyes flicking briefly over her short housecoat. Either by accident or by devious intention, he had selected the sexiest nightgown and robe she owned. The plunging neckline and sheer clinging material scarcely went past her thighs, making the outfit almost indecent to walk around in. With a barely concealed smirk he went back to scrubbing the dog.

"Feeling better, Auntie Erin?" he asked breezily.

"A little." She clutched the front of her gown closer to her, a bit disconcerted that he was still around. Her eyes followed his quick, efficient movements with the dog. "Price, what are you doing?" she asked, stepping closer to get a better look at the dog.

"It seems Huntley, our little pal there in the glasses, didn't care for the color of ole E.T., so he decided to paint him green. Real eye-catching, isn't it?" Price said, standing up to display the wet, gummy, shivering green dog.

"Huntley!" Erin scolded, looking at him in disapproval. "Didn't I tell you to stay out of that paint yesterday?"

"You said I couldn't paint my *name* on the garage door, Aunt Erin. You didn't say nothin' about the dog," he rationalized calmly, taking another bite of his apple.

"Well, no problem," Price said, pouring more paint remover on the rag. "E.T. may look a little strange to all his girlfriends for a while, but they'll probably think it's some kinky new fashion dogs are wearing nowadays."

Erin was amazed at the patience Price seemed to have with the children. In her opinion, he would have been the last person in the world to take this type of thing so calmly.

"I didn't think you were still here," she murmured quietly, her gaze fastening on his large hands as he gently massaged the paint off the white fur.

"And where did you think I would go?" he teased lightly, "with two five-year-olds, one sick aunt, one green dog and two dead goldfish?"

Erin glanced worriedly over at the twins. "So you know about—that?"

"I know about that," he said, wrapping a thick, fleecy towel around E.T. "Holly thought she saw some dirt on Cinderella's face, so she decided to give her and Buck a long-overdue bath." Price winked at Erin secretly. "To Holly's knowledge they hadn't had one in quite some time. They were both naturally quite upset to find out that fish don't take baths, but I managed to explain that accidents happen and Buck and Cinderella probably enjoyed their bubble bath . . . as long as they could." He sat the dog back down on the floor and began to rub powder into its furry body. "We thought that after you woke up, we'd have the—deceaseds' funeral. Then, if you felt like it, we'd all go down to the pet store for some new fish."

"Buck Wogers and Cindewella have gone to the big fish hatchewy in the sky," Holly explained sadly. "They're much happier now, Aunt Erin, so don't feel bad."

Erin bit her lip painfully as she tried to keep a straight face. Huntley's and Holly's features were tragic masks of composure, trying to bear up under the heavy burden Holly was carrying.

"Well, I'm happy to say I *am* feeling better, and I certainly wouldn't want to miss services for Buck and Cinderella," Erin said succinctly, turning her head away from their mournful gazes. Her eyes met Price's amused

49

ones as they both grinned knowingly at each other. "Who's giving the eulogy?" she asked sweetly.

"Reverend Seaver's been preparing notes all afternoon, ma'am," he said proudly, finally releasing the squirming dog. E.T. stood in the middle of the floor and shook his body two or three times, then began to roll on a small area rug that was lying next to his bed, trying to assuage the terrific itching from all the bath and powder he had just been subjected to.

"Really." She smiled delightedly. "I can hardly wait for the sermon! It must not be easy to find something—really special to say about two—fish." She had to bite her lip again as Price continued to grin mockingly back at her. "I mean, two fish you barely knew," she finished lamely, averting her eyes from his before she burst out laughing.

"On the contrary, some of my most stirring sermons have been given at funerals for pets," he stated smugly as he cleaned up the last remains of the paint-stained rags. "If I were you I'd go slip into something more"—his emerald gaze skipped suggestively over her skimpy gown —"conservative. Not that I don't find your attire extremely appealing, but I'm afraid the neighbors might talk," he finished, bringing his mouth close to her ear in a whisper. Shivers of delight raced through Erin's skin as his lips brushed her ear softly before turning back to the twins. "Let's go, guys. You go get the matchbox while I dig a grave site. Aunt Erin will join us out in the backyard as soon as she is dressed."

They ran off obediently to their task, leaving Price and Erin standing in the small utility room. Shyness overtook Erin as she realized that they were alone. "Price, I thought you were going to find someone to come and stay until I felt better," she reminded him, averting her eyes from his glance hurriedly.

"I tried a couple of people, but I couldn't find anyone who could stay more than one day," he replied casually, adding, "Oh, by the way, the plumber came and got the ball out of the toilet. I decided that since I'm not on any rigid schedule right now, I can hang around for a few days. Have you got any big objections to that?" His eyes finally managed to catch hers.

"What about your job?" Erin struggled to find an excuse for him not to stay.

Price gave an ironic chuckle. "Since I own my own company in Memphis, I don't think they're going to say too much. Seaver Trucking will go on for a few days whether I'm there or not."

"Aren't you rather young to have your own trucking company?" she asked in surprise.

"I'm thirty-two, Erin. I've always worked very hard for things that are important to me," he said mildly, his eyes reluctant to leave hers. "I'd be happy to stay a day or two to help you."

"That's really not necessary, Price," she answered curtly, pushing her way around him to walk into the larger space off the kitchen. His closeness unnerved her. "I'm sure you have someone waiting for you at home. I'm really feeling much better now." The thought had suddenly struck her that she didn't know if Price was married.

Price followed her into the kitchen, then leaned against the kitchen sink, crossing his arms in amusement. "Just the normal two or three hundred good-looking, ravishing women who trail me around constantly," he taunted with a devious sparkle in his green eyes. "But a man gets tired of seeing all those beautiful faces gazing at him adoringly day in and day out. I thought it might be refreshing to stay around here a few days and just gaze on you awhile."

His cocky smile infuriated her. She knew he was deliberately trying to antagonize her, playing on her insecurities.

"You may think that's very funny, Price, but I don't," she said coolly, itching to slap his face. "I may not be a

51

raving beauty, but I'm not that bad. I could attract a man if I wanted to."

Price's face grew serious as his arms dropped to his sides. "Well, well, well," he said quietly. "I was beginning to get worried about you, lady. Is it possible that you've finally taken your sackcloth and ashes off and looked in the mirror?"

"I'm sure I don't have the slightest idea what you're talking about, Price. If you mean do I realize that I'm not as unattractive as I've been babbling on about lately, then the answer is yes." Her voice was defiant as she glared back into Price's taunting eyes.

"I couldn't agree more," he said quietly. "I'd even take it a step further and admit that you're a damn appealing woman. But I suppose that's hoping for a little too much, isn't it?" he added sarcastically.

Barely aware of her actions, Erin reached out and slapped him hard across his cheek. Price's stunned look frightened her.

He instantly grabbed her hand and jerked her up close against his broad chest. Their angry eyes locked as he said from between clenched teeth, "Don't you *ever* try that again, lady. I've about had it up to here with you," he threatened in a grim voice.

"You touch me and I'll scream," she vowed hotly, trying to twist out of his iron grip. "What do you want from me!"

"Scream—see if I give a damn," he said in a controlled voice. "What you need is a man to take control of you, Erin. Someone who'll take you to bed several times a day until he proves to you that you're a desirable woman." His voice had grown husky now as he drew her angry face up next to his. "Someone who can make you *love* for a change, instead of feeling sorry for yourself."

"I'm not interested in a man—not just any man, that is," she whispered hotly.

"And what's that supposed to mean?" Price returned irritably.

"I mean I am interested in a man, but I haven't found the perf—the right one yet."

"I believe you started to say the 'perfect' one, didn't you?" Price kept her trapped against his chest, his soft breath fanning her face. "I hate to be the bearer of bad news, Erin, but if you'll pardon the expression, there ain't no such creature."

"I refuse to believe that. Look at Nathan—he's the perfect man, and he and Brenda have the perfect marriage. He totally adores the ground she walks on, and she returns that love. If I thought for one moment that I wouldn't be able to find that kind of man in my life, well, I think I would just give up. Especially after Quinn. . . ." Her voice trailed off quietly.

"Quinn? I suppose he's the guy that's got me in so much hot water?"

Erin sighed and pushed away from Price to walk to the kitchen window. She stared out at the twins as they played near their sandbox, waiting for the funeral. How could she tell Price, a man who reminded her so much of Quinn— yet Erin was beginning to see that they were really nothing alike at all—just how much Quinn Daniels had hurt her without sounding like she was feeling sorry for herself again.

"Quinn Daniels was a man I thought I loved very deeply—a man whom I dreamed of having the perfect marriage with ever since I was nineteen years old. I'm afraid I'm a person whose dreams die hard, Price. I want a per—good marriage. When I found out six months ago that I would never have that marriage with Quinn, I decided that I would not let that turn me bitter and disillusioned. Somewhere out there in the world there is a man who wants the kind of marriage I do, and I'm going to find him. It may take months, years, maybe a lifetime, but I will find him, Price. In spite of Quinn Daniels."

"Quinn Daniels! Nathan's brother?" Price's face showed surprise.

"That's right. I'm sure you know him if you know Nathan."

"I've met him a couple of times. Why would you fall for a romeo like him? You look like you'd have more common sense than that."

Erin gave a shaky laugh and sat down on the kitchen chair. "I've asked myself the same question over and over. My only consolation is the fact that I wasn't the only one. Quinn attracts girls like watermelon attracts flies!" She smiled up sheepishly at Price. "I know you think I've acted horribly—and I have. Please forgive me. It's just that I've had such a terrible headache, and the twins have been more than a handful since I got here—"

"You don't have to apologize," Price interrupted gently. "I knew that things weren't exactly going your way." He smiled. "And if it makes you feel any better, I know what you went through with Quinn." His eyes became pained, their lovely green growing dark and still. "If things had turned out differently, I wouldn't be within a hundred miles of here tonight. I would be a married man, spending a nice quiet night alone with my new wife."

Erin's eyes flew up to meet his, her heart giving an unusual lurch. For some reason the thought of Price being married suddenly upset her.

"Like you, I thought I had found the perfect woman. But it seems we didn't see eye to eye on a lot of things, so she found someone who let her have her way all the time." For the first time Erin heard bitterness creep into Price's voice.

"Did you love her?"

Price glanced at her in exasperation. "Of course I loved her! Do you think I'd marry someone I didn't love?"

"No. I just meant—did you love her a lot?"

"If you mean did it hurt like hell when she left me, yes, Erin, it hurt."

"I know. That's how I felt when I broke off with Quinn six months ago," Erin said sympathetically.

"Six months ago? Funny, that's when Jeannie and I broke up."

"Really, that *is* funny." They both sat staring at the sugar bowl on the kitchen table, each one lost in thought.

"Well, there's no use rehashing old memories. The past is—past. I made up my mind that I'm cut out to be a bachelor, anyway. It probably would never have worked out, and Jeannie just saw it quicker than I did. Look, I know we got off to a bad start, but if you're willing, I'd like to be your friend." His celadon gaze met hers with sincerity.

He wanted to be her friend! Erin mulled the unexpected suggestion over in her mind, then rejected it silently. Somehow she had the distinct impression that it would be extremely hard to be just a friend to such a virile, totally masculine man as Price Seaver. But if he wanted to think they could be friends, what harm could it do?

"Thank you, Price, that's very nice of you."

"One thing that should help console both of us is the fact that we can be just ourselves. I know *I'm* not looking for another involvement with a woman for a long time—if ever. And you're not likely to find your perfect man in the next few days. So how about my giving you a hand with the twins until Brenda and Nathan get back? I'm long overdue for a vacation."

"It won't be much of a vacation," Erin warned with a frown. "I'm nearly exhausted after only two days!"

"Well," Price said with another disarming grin in her direction, "it's bound to be easier with two."

"Oh, Price." Erin hung her head in shame, thinking of

how rude she had been to him since they had met. "I wish you wouldn't be so nice."

"Why not? It looks to me like it was past time a man was nice to you. You asked me what I wanted from you, Erin. My answer is nothing. I'm afraid Jeannie has spoiled my outlook on marriage and women in general for a long time to come. But if there's a perfect man out there, I hope you find him. It seems to me you deserve one."

"I think Jeannie must have been a little crazy," Erin said truthfully.

"That's funny, I was thinking the same thing about Quinn. So it's agreed; we'll be friends. I'll stick around and help with the twins for a few days, get in a little fishing, relax for a while, then I'll head back to Memphis."

"If you're sure that's how you want to spend your vacation. I must admit I could use the help." Erin paused. "I'd sincerely like to be your friend, Price—but nothing more." The whole idea suddenly seemed ridiculous. Surely he wasn't serious.

Price looked amused. "I'm not asking for anything but a few days away from the rat race, Erin. I haven't been with a woman in the last six months, so I think I'll be able to struggle through the next few days without endangering our—friendship."

Erin's heart fell. Well, holy cow! He *was* serious! "In that case, welcome aboard—friend!" Erin stuck out her hand and placed it in his large one, fighting an overwhelming surge of disappointment.

Price gripped her hand tightly, his smile growing broader. "Thanks—friend. Now I believe we have a funeral service to attend."

The intoning voice of "Reverend Seaver" held the attention of the small gathering under the tall spreading oak. Each one in his or her own special way was there to mourn the passing of Buck Rogers and Cinderella Fish. The two

56

littlest mourners stood clutching the reassuring hand of the pretty woman who stood next to the small grave site, their round eyes fixed solidly on the small cardboard box lying beside the gaping hole that read Lights Every Time matches. Erin listened reverently as Price praised the unquestionable goodness of Buck and Cinderella. Commenting that they had bubbled less than the ordinary goldfish he had known and never grew upset when they were not fed regularly, he reassured the mourners that Buck and Cinderella had a much stronger constitution than the average goldfish. Price cited as example the time Buck had lay on the coffee table for the better part of one whole afternoon when Huntley had taken him out to speak personally to him, then forgot to replace him in the bowl when his mother had called him to lunch. His comforting voice reminded Holly that Cinderella would be the cleanest fish up there, able to boast of having had a fragrant, delightful bubble bath just prior to her—long journey.

Price said a short prayer over the remains, then stuck the matchbox down into the small grave and covered it quickly with dirt. Holly stepped forward and placed a small clump of the flowers that still bloomed wild all over the banks of the lake this time of year on the lump of fresh dirt. With one long racking sigh the twins turned away from the grave site and walked morosely back toward the house.

"Hey." Price whistled shrilly. "Have you shown your aunt Erin what your dad and I built you this winter?"

Their faces lit up immediately, all gloomy thoughts dispelled as their eyes looked past Erin to a platform built about five feet off the ground on a limb of the old oak tree.

"Our tree house," they shouted joyfully. They flashed past Erin in a rush as they ran toward the tree, climbing carefully up on the small wooden ladder hooked to the platform.

"What is this?" Erin questioned, her eyes taking in the

large tree house the twins had crawled up into. It was built low to the ground, so they could easily get into it, and would present no dangers if they should become careless and tumble out. A neat thatched roof covered the large platform that had been thoughtfully covered with straw for tender knees to crawl around on. It made the perfect place to play on hot summer afternoons, a perfectly enchanting hideaway overlooking the sparkling blue waters of the lake.

"It's our very own house that Daddy and Uncle Price built," Huntley told her proudly. "You wanna come up here and sit in it for a while, Aunt Erin?" he invited graciously. "Boy, is it neat!"

Price came to stand behind her as she shaded her eyes to peer up into the tree. "No, I'll just stay down here and watch you. Be careful!" she added as she watched a minor skirmish develop between the two over territorial rights.

"Don't you want to climb up there and take a look at the view? It's spectacular," Price whispered from behind her. "Remind me to take you up there some moonlit night before you leave." He grinned at her suggestively, adding, "Friend."

"Did you help build this?" She smiled in admiration, noting that the tree house wasn't some flimsily constructed piece of work. It apparently had been well thought out and built with care.

"Designed it and helped build it," Price said, looking at the structure with pride. "Nathan and I always did want one of these things when we were kids, so one day we just decided to buy the wood and start building! Do you really like it?" he asked eagerly.

If Erin had hated it, she wouldn't have had the heart to tell him so. He was looking at her so proudly, that little-boy look surfacing on his face. But she didn't hate it—it was simply lovely and she hurriedly told him so.

The twins played happily for another five minutes while

Erin wandered around the area, breathing in the clean air. In the far distance she could see the white sails of several boats bobbing along on the sparkling waters. Everything seemed so peaceful—so perfect. Her gaze involuntarily sought out Price as he laughed and played with the twins in their tree house, his dark, wavy hair ruffling in the light breeze. With sudden clarity she knew that he could present a real danger to her. Nothing had ever frightened her more as that moment when she realized he was *not* Quinn. She paused, drinking in the sight of him, vowing to fight those feelings.

Price glanced up from his rowdy scuffling with Huntley and flashed her one of those devastating grins. They both waved at her boisterously, motioning for her to come up and join them. Erin smiled and waved back, starting the climb up the small embankment she had wandered down. Her hands were full of the summer flowers that blanketed the hillsides. Holly ran down to greet her, and they walked hand in hand up the hill to meet the men. Price smiled down at her as they joined them, his arm slipping around her waist as they proceeded on up the grassy rise leading to the house. To the casual onlooker they would present a picture of the perfect happy family—Mother, Daddy and children. Only the tall, handsome man holding the petite, curly brown-headed woman's hand and she knew it was a false image.

"Still feel like a hamburger?" Price asked casually, matching his strides to her smaller ones.

"Do you know what you're letting yourself in for?" she warned laughingly. "The twins' table manners are, shall we say, extremely lax."

Price ceased walking and turned to face her condescendingly, placing his hand smugly on his lean hips. "Now do I look like the kind of man who would let two five-year-olds get the best of him?"

Erin bit back a grin as she surveyed his perfectly tailored brown designer jeans and his light brown striped oxford shirt. Price gave the appearance that he had just stepped out of a fashion magazine. He had the kind of suave sophistication that would enable him to look like a million dollars in a gunny sack. Somehow she didn't think he knew what he was letting himself in for this time.

"Well, I'm game if you are, Mr. Seaver," she said fatalistically.

"You've just got to know how to handle these kids," he reasoned sensibly as they all walked up to his new, sparkling clean car. "You have to tell children what's expected of them and then enforce it." He opened the door and the twins exploded into the backseat, their shoes leaving dust marks across the plush gray upholstery where they had walked. A funny look flooded his face as he glanced up sheepishly at Erin and reached over frantically to dust off the scuff marks. "Now you guys keep your feet on the floor," he instructed patiently, grabbing hold of one of Huntley's gouging feet. "Uncle Price gets *real* upset when you put your dirty shoes on the seats," he added nicely.

The twins immediately ceased their squirming and put their feet obediently on the floor. Price shot Erin an I-told-you-so smirk as he held the door open for her on the passenger side.

"Very impressive," she said, snickering under her breath. "You *do* have a way with a five-year-old." She couldn't wait till feeding time!

On the ride to McDonald's, the power windows in the backseat flapped up and down like window shades as Price's expensive car sped along the highway. Erin kept her face averted, gazing out the car window and pushing back her giggles as Price worriedly tolerated the windows zipping up and down. By the time they pulled into the parking lot of the restaurant, Huntley had managed to squeeze his tiny fingers between Price's seat, nimbly finding the master-control box. All four windows were buzzing up and down at the same time as Erin looked at Price sweetly. "When are you going to tell them what's expected of them?"

Price switched the engine off and turned to grab Huntley's plundering hands. "All right, you guys, let's knock it off! Huntley, let go of that switch!"

Holly set up a screech as Erin removed her hands from the once-clean glass of the back window. A smeary palm print was definitely visible. Erin glanced uneasily at Price.

"Okay, now what does everyone want to eat?" Price asked after calm was finally restored to the inside of the car.

"Are we going to eat in the car?" Erin asked in amazement.

"Don't you think we can—watch them a little closer out here?" Price asked worriedly.

"But your beautiful car. . . ." Erin's eyes surveyed the immaculate plush interior of the car. Letting the twins eat in here would be like throwing slops to a hog.

"I'd rather keep an eye on them in here than try to keep up with them in there." His eyes motioned toward the crowded dining room.

"It's your car," Erin said hesitantly. "I'll have a cheeseburger, french fries and a small Coke." She paused, thinking about her extra ten pounds. "Forget my french fries and make that a sugar-free drink. Get the children 'happy meals.' "

Price gave her a suggestive look. "No fries and a sugar-free *small* drink. I gather you're thinking about your figure again," he teased gently. "Since we're only friends, don't worry about those extra pounds and have a decent meal. You haven't eaten since last night."

"No thank you. Just the hamburger and drink."

"Suit yourself," he said resignedly. "What am I supposed to get the kids?"

"Get them 'happy meals,' " she repeated. "Just trust me, Price. They really do serve such things."

"They'd better or it's your neck," he warned with a grimace, stepping out of the car. "If I go loping up there and ask for two 'happy meals' and she looks at me as if I just rode in with a bus full of crazies, you'll pay, lady."

Within ten minutes he was back, his arms loaded with drinks and sandwiches. Erin made the twins sit quietly in the backseat while she spread napkins in their laps and carefully laid out their hamburgers and fries.

"Now be very careful and don't spill *anything* on Uncle Price's nice clean car," she cautioned, eyeing them warily.

"We won't!" They both began to devour their dinners hungrily.

Price and Erin munched contentedly on their hamburgers, exchanging smalltalk as the backseat remained calm. During one of the pauses in conversation, the distinct sound of a drink turning over, the ice sloshing onto the mats on the floor, reached their ears. Erin paused in her chewing and glanced at Price.

"Don't worry about it. I'll clean it up later," he said under his breath. "As long as they're quiet, let's not stir up a hornets' nest!"

Erin shrugged her shoulders and took another bite of her hamburger.

"Do you got any ketchup, Uncle Pwice?" Holly asked through a mouth full of hamburger.

"Do I have any ketchup," Price corrected, reaching for a plastic package lying between the seats.

"That's what I said," she replied crossly.

"Here, what do you want it on?" Price turned in his seat to help her.

"My fwench fwies. I'll do it!" She held out her chubby hand to receive the ketchup.

"I don't think so, Holly. You let *me* put it on your fries," Price said in a no-nonsense tone, visions of huge red blotches of ketchup on his gray upholstery appearing sickly in his head.

Holly plopped back in the seat disgustedly, knocking her soda over this time.

"Damn." Price groaned under his breath, squeezing out the last of the ketchup on Holly's fries. "I'd better clean both of those sodas up before they start wallowing in them."

"Here, let me help you . . ." Erin's words stuck in her throat; she watched in horror as the drink that was sitting between them tipped over and spilled in his lap. Price sucked in his breath, then sprang out of the car like a scalded cat, holding the front of his pants away from his drenched skin. Erin froze in her seat, not quite certain what to do. Price hopped beside the car for a few minutes, doing what Erin considered an admirable job of not coming unglued.

"I'm sorry," she said in a small voice, leaning over his seat to peek out the door at him. "Is there anything I can do?"

"Nothing," he said tightly, reaching for the back floor mats and dumping the ice and dirty cola on the ground. The twins stood up on the seat and watched in silent fascination as Price tried to restore some semblance of order to the car.

Erin reached over and laid Holly's fries on the driver's seat and brushed some stray crumbs off her seat. Poor Price, she thought worriedly, his car will never look the same!

."Boy, Aunt Erin sure made a mess, huh?" Huntley observed from behind his large glasses, one french fry stuck casually between his fingers like a cigarette.

Price looked up at him blandly. "Why don't you eat that french fry instead of smoking it, chum."

After brushing off the front of his jeans one more time, he opened the door and slid back into the driver's side. A frantic scream spewed out of Holly as Price came up out of his seat rapidly. "What's the matter now?" he bellowed, turning to glower at her hostilely.

"You sat on my fwench fwies and ketchup," she wailed, glaring back at him defiantly.

"Ohhhh—oh—shoot!" Price shouted, leaping out of the car and fighting to control his language in front of the children.

The twins watched in wide-eyed absorption as Price irritably picked Holly's ketchup-covered french fries off his not-so-immaculate brown jeans.

Glancing up, he saw the look of terror on all three faces. With a mean scowl on his face, he picked up some fries that were lying on the ground minus the ketchup. With great stalking strides he paced his way slowly to the car door, a growl coming from his throat.

Huntley swallowed hard and blinked back at him through his horn-rim glasses. Holly, never brave to begin with, cowered against Erin, her eyes round as saucers.

Price leered in the car door and said in a deep gruff voice, "Who put the fwench fwies in my seat!" "Was it you?" He looked straight at Holly, his eyes piercing her uneasy brown ones. She shook her head, scared. "Was it you?" he asked Huntley. The other twin swallowed hard again and shook his head nervously.

Price crawled over the seat and pressed his face up against Erin's in an exaggerated angry stance. "Then it was you!" he accused righteously.

"Yeah, want to make something out of it?" She grinned saucily.

Amid peals of relieved laughter, Price lunged at Erin, getting her down in the car seat and stuffing the french fries he carried down her blouse. The twins piled on top of him, and the car erupted in one big tickling match, squeals of laughter filling the air.

Price's hand came up under Erin's blouse and touched

one of her breasts playfully, then lingered there for a moment. Erin shot him a dirty glare as he shrugged fatalistically before removing it discreetly.

"I *thought* we were going to be friends," Erin hissed sharply under her breath.

"We are! Wasn't I being friendly enough?" he asked innocently.

"You're being too friendly," she muttered, pushing his large bulk off her, sending the twins into new fits of giggles.

"Maybe we should reconsider this friend theory," he shouted above the chattering voices of the twins as they tried to restore some order to their dinner. "And then again, maybe we shouldn't." He grinned as Erin shot him a dirty look.

By the time they had settled themselves back down and drove out of the parking lot, Price's car would have sold for half the price he had paid for it six months earlier. Erin glanced at his masculine profile as they pulled onto the highway. They had had so much fun today. Would it be this way when she found her perfect man? Of course it would! And for the first time in a very long time, Erin couldn't wait to start looking for him again. She looked at Price out of the corner of her eye. Reconsider their friendship? Never! Well . . . at least not now, anyway.

CHAPTER FOUR

By the time they arrived home, the twins and Erin were feeling the effects of the day. And Price was irritable and eager to get out of his ruined pants. The twins became crankier by the minute, and Erin's head still bore faint traces of her migraine. With Price's help, she soon had both children bathed and was helping Holly get ready for bed.

"I wanted to wear my yellow jammies," Holly fretted as Erin brushed her damp, baby-sweet-smelling locks out of her face.

"Your yellow pajamas are dirty, Holly. Remember, you wore them the first night I was here," Erin reminded her patiently, giving her another hug.

Chubby arms went around Erin's neck and squeezed tight as Holly kissed her aunt lovingly. "I wove you, Aunt Erin."

"I love you, too, Holly."

"When's Mommy and Daddy coming home? I miss them." Holly's big brown eyes grew misty. A week was a long time to a five-year-old.

"In another few days. Now that I'm feeling better, maybe we can go on a picnic or see a movie. Would you like that?"

"How long's a few days?" she persisted, her arms wrapping tighter around Erin's neck.

"Now, let's see . . . your mommy and daddy left Sunday. Today is Tuesday. Do you know the days of the week?"

Holly shook her head woefully. "No, but I can count to five."

"Well, if you can count to five, you know that you have five fingers on your hand. See!" Erin picked up her hand and pointed to each of her fingers. "Now we're going to hide your thumb, and in the morning we'll hide this finger, then the next day we'll hide another finger, and when we've hidden all your fingers but this little teeny one"— Erin wiggled a fat little finger playfully, eliciting a squeal of delight from Holly—"then the next day your mommy and daddy come home!"

Holly stopped giggling and looked down at her hand solemnly. She wiggled her little finger experimentally, hiding the other four. Looking up, she bestowed a radiant smile on Erin and said, "That won't be very wong, will it?"

"No, not very long at all. Now why don't you run on out and see if Price has Huntley ready for bed."

When Erin and Holly reached the front room, Price was in the process of buttoning a squirming Huntley's pajamas. They were a loud color of red, with MACHO MUNCH-KIN written across the front.

"Hold on, macho," Price commanded as he fought to get the last button fastened. "Boy, you need a road map to get into these things," he told Erin with a frown. "Why do they put so many buttons on a kid's pajamas?"

"I don't know. I think they have one lone crazy man sitting up in a tower somewhere working for all the children's clothing companies, and his job is to design clothes that take hours to get in and out of." Erin laughed as she sat down next to him on the couch.

The twins scrambled between them, fighting over who got to sit next to Uncle Price.

Price and Erin each took a twin in their laps and snuggled down deeper in the sofa to relax before they carted them off to bed. Huntley poked his finger into the beak of his slipper and made an exaggerated pretense of being bitten by the yellow bird.

"Don't you wish you had some slippers like these, Uncle Price?" he asked after his antics failed to get any response out of the older couple.

Price eyed the colorful birds for a moment. "Yeah, I was just sitting here thinking that you had all the luck. Where did you get those things?"

"Santa Kwaus brought them to him," Holly butted in. "He brought me mine, too. See!" She stuck her foot in Price's face.

"Yes, they are sure nice. Don't you wish we had a pair of bird slippers like those, Aunt Erin?" Price asked with a twinkle in his eye.

"Maybe Santa will bring you a pair," Erin encouraged playfully.

"Yeah, but you better put it on your list," Huntley warned. "You only get three things from Santa Claus." He bolted from Price's lap and ran to grab the pad and pencil lying next to the phone, returning to his seat instantly. "I'm going to write down my three things right now!"

"A little early, isn't it, chum?" Price stilled his kicking feet hurriedly. "Christmas isn't for another four months yet."

"I don't care. I might forget." He fixed his mouth in a thoughtful grimace, then began to write in big, bold letters. TRAIN, DUMS, B.B. GUM. "Here, Uncle Price, you read it and be sure I spelled everything all right." He shoved the paper at his uncle.

Price took the slip of paper and read aloud. "Let's see, you want a train, a—dum—"

"Drum!"

"Oh, right, a drum and a—oh, mercy!" He groaned under his breath, then continued, "A BB gun. Right?"

"Right!"

"They'd have to declare the neighborhood a disaster area if ole Santa comes through with this list," Price said, grinning at Erin.

"Help me write down what I want, Aunt Ewin." Holly jerked the pad and pencil out of Huntley's hand.

Huntley reached over and pinched her soundly before Price could jerk his hand away.

"This kid is faster than a speedin' bullet," Price said with a groan as Holly let out an earsplitting scream.

"Holly! That's enough! Now quiet down and tell me what you want me to write on your list," Erin said sternly.

The wails immediately ceased. "I want a lellow bicycle, a doll that wets, and uh . . . a ten-dollar bill."

"Now there's a girl after my own heart," Price said happily.

Erin looked at him teasingly. "Do you want me to write down your list, Price?"

"No. Give me the pad and pencil. I'll write my own." He wiggled his brows at Huntley smugly. "We don't want those silly women writing out our list, do we?"

Huntley began to bounce up and down. "What do you want, Uncle Price?"

"Well, now, let me think. I think I'll take a . . . lellow Maserati." He paused and made a big pretense of thinking. "I definitely don't want a doll that wets her pants." He winked at Erin suggestively. "But I would take the ten-dollar bill, and since I only have one gift left . . . that will have to be the bird slippers."

"Yeah, yeah, okay, now it's your turn, Aunt Erin!" the twins chorused.

"Oh, dear, I really don't know. I'd like to have a diamond ring, a mink coat, and . . ." She rolled her eyes upward, studying the ceiling.

"And a perfect marriage," Price finished her list for her.

Erin looked startled for a moment, then said softly,

69

"Yes, I would like that. A diamond ring, a mink coat—and a perfect marriage."

"Yuk! I hope Santa Claus doesn't get our gifts mixed up," Huntley said adamantly. "I want my drums!"

"And I think it's time both you little munchkins were in bed," Price announced as he rose from the couch with a twin under each arm. "Aunt Erin, why don't you fix us some iced tea while I tuck these rug rats into bed."

"Do you need any help?" Erin rose to her feet and started to follow him.

"Nope, I can handle this all by myself. You just get the iced tea."

"Night, Aunt Erin." The twins giggled.

"I'll be in to kiss you later, okay?" she called.

Price stopped and shifted his bundles more evenly. "You talking to me?"

Erin blushed. "No, I meant the twins!"

"Darn! Huntley gets the bird slippers and kisses too!" he grumbled good-naturedly as he disappeared down the hall.

By the time he returned, Erin had two large glasses of iced tea waiting. Price walked back into the room and took a seat on the sofa next to her, stretching out his tall frame in weary relief. "I think they fell asleep before their heads hit the pillow."

"You're very good with them," Erin commented as she handed him his glass, then laid her head back on the sofa and closed her eyes.

"Yeah, well, I love kids. I always thought I'd like to have four or five. I suppose I'm getting a little old for that many now."

"Oh, I don't think so. You still have plenty of time," Erin said softly.

"Well, maybe. Jeannie didn't want children. At least not right away." He stared into the cold fireplace, his mind drifting. "Not that it matters now one way or the other."

70

They sat in easy, relaxed companionship, sipping their iced teas. The house grew hushed and a sense of peacefulness washed over the couple in the small family room. Erin could see the moon reflecting off the still waters of the lake through the large glass window on the west side of the wall.

"Do you have any brothers or sisters?" Price asked conversationally.

"No, I'm an only child. I always wanted brothers and sisters, though." She laughed. "When we were making out our Christmas lists earlier, it brought to mind how I always used to start in around the first of October telling Mom and Dad that I only wanted a brother or a sister for my Christmas present. Nothing else—just a brother or a sister."

"I gather your parents decided to go along with the usual dolls and roller skates?"

"Yes." Erin smiled. "It wasn't until I reached womanhood myself that Mom told me they had never been able to have other children. In fact, they considered me a miracle child."

"That's too bad. . . . I come from a fairly large family. I have two brothers and two sisters," Price said quietly, deep in thought. "I used to come home from school every day to a house that smelled like fresh-baked cookies, pot roast, and a mom who met me at the door with a bear hug."

"I had the same thing," Erin murmured, "only I used to get so lonely. All the other kids had big brothers to protect them or sisters to argue with over clothes or boyfriends. All I had was a stuffed rabbit I used to take to bed with me every night and tell my troubles to."

"What troubles?" Price grinned affectionately. "Things like how you were the homeliest girl in the class—"

"No, I wasn't!" Erin stopped him curtly. "I was a cute *little* girl."

71

"Really? Well"—he leaned back and took another sip of his iced tea—"I was just sitting here thinking you aren't half bad now that you're all grown up."

Erin punched him playfully. "Thanks. Are you trying to tell me God doesn't make junk?"

"In your case, he didn't." Price winked. "At least the parts I've seen."

Erin blushed, her mind flashing back to when he had undressed her the other night. Price had seen everything there was to see of Erin Holmes. Her heart lifted at the thought that he had liked what he saw.

"Do you still take your rabbit to bed with you at night?"

"For lack of something better, yes." Erin grinned at him wickedly.

"Such a waste." Price shook his head regretfully, his eyes running over her feminine softness lazily. "Some rabbits have all the luck."

"I want children," Erin said, quickly turning the subject back to their previous discussion. "I used to think I wanted eight."

"Eight!" Price nearly choked on his drink. "Good grief, woman, you'd better marry a rabbit!"

Erin grinned happily. "You wouldn't want eight?"

"I hardly think so! In fact, I'm beginning to think that wanting five is bordering on insanity! Can you imagine eight Huntleys running amuck in this world?"

"Oh, my children are not going to be like the twins. They're going to be perfect," Erin said proudly.

Price watched the soft lamplight play over her lovely features. "Naturally. Perfect marriages *would* have perfect children," he said softly.

Erin opened her eyes and looked at him for a moment. "Are you teasing me about that?"

"No," he replied tiredly, leaning his head back now and staring up at the ceiling. "It's just that I hate to see you get hurt a second time, Erin."

"Hurt—what do you mean by that?"

"There is no perfect marriage, Erin. There's no perfect man; no perfect woman. Surely you realize that."

Erin sighed and closed her eyes again. "I can always dream, can't I?"

"As long as you realize that everything has its share of problems, and you don't go running through life looking for something that isn't there and never will be."

"What's wrong with wanting what other people have? Nathan and Brenda—"

"Nathan has had more than his share of problems, Erin. Hasn't Brenda mentioned to you that Nathan was married once before?"

Erin's eyes flew open. "What!"

"I thought you knew that. He's never made a secret of it. It was one of those crazy teenage marriages that lasted about two months. After the divorce he went into the service. He didn't meet Brenda until after his discharge."

"But Quinn never mentioned that to me." Erin was totally dumbfounded.

"Apparently Quinn didn't mention a number of things to you," Price said pointedly. "Nathan and Brenda's marriage, I'm sure, is far from perfect. In fact, I can think of two prime examples lying right in the next room!"

"That's not a good example! They love those children dearly," Erin exclaimed indignantly.

"I know they do, but I've also heard them go around and around over any discipline Nathan wants to dole out."

"At least Nathan isn't out chasing every pretty skirt in town like his brother is," Erin grumbled. "At least he's home every night with his wife and unruly children!"

"Yeah, he *is* a good husband. Good—not perfect!"

"I don't care what you say, Price. When I marry, it will be to a man who will be completely devoted to me and our children. He'll spend every night home with me, we'll do things together, we won't need other people in our lives, he will never look at another woman—we will never quarrel, and I will make his life perfect."

"Damn, I feel sorry for the poor man already!"

"Why? Isn't that the way a marriage should be? Don't you wish Jeannie would have thought a little more along those lines?"

"Leave Jeannie out of this," Price snapped.

"Why, because you still love her?" Erin pressed. "Don't you want a wife who needs only you and no one else?"

"Yes, but I don't want to live in a cell block! My wife *will* need only me, but she'll love me enough not to smother me to death. What you just described is a prison, not a healthy marriage!"

Erin's eyes began to water with unshed tears. "I didn't mean that we couldn't have other friends. I just meant—" Her voice broke as the tears started streaming down her face. "I just meant I didn't want my husband to be thinking of other women. I want to be the only woman in his life—the only one who lies in his arms at night. . . ."

Price moved toward her, and his hand reached out to pull her face against his broad chest as he whispered softly into the fragrance of her curly hair. "And you have every right to expect that from the man you love, Erin, whether it's your husband or not. I didn't mean that a marriage couldn't have all the ingredients you just listed and still be a damn good one. I only want you to see that you can't have a perfect one, because you'll go on searching until you're old and gray, and you'll never find it, honey. Quinn Daniels was no good and he's left a lot of scars in your life. You won't find a perfect man, but they won't all be Quinns either."

The tears fell harder as she pressed against him, his warmth and presence more than comforting. It had been such a very long time since she had opened up her heart and let anyone see just how deep her hurt was. The cleansing tears continued to fall, dampening the front of Price's

74

shirt. Words failed him as he held her sobbing form in his arms. What could he say? If he could have gotten the words past the lump in his throat, he would probably have told her that he had shed his own share of tears in the last few months. He had felt frustrated, and so deeply resentful of Jeannie that he thought life just plain stank and saw no purpose for going on. But he had buried his hurt and faced one day at a time. The only logical way to keep from being hurt like that again was never to become involved—deeply involved—with a woman again. If he could help Erin see that she would never find a perfect marriage—or a perfect man—then he could save her a lot of hurt in the future.

Erin's softness pressed into Price's body, and his arms tightened around her automatically. Six months; it had been six long months since he had held a woman in his arms, kissed her, smelled the fragrance of her hair. When Jeannie left, he hadn't wanted to think about a woman, let alone be with one. He knew lots of men who tried to kill the pain with other women or a bottle, but he had never been that type. Sex was not a casual thing to him, at least sex without some type of commitment. But his body seemed to know how long it had been since he had made love to a woman, as he became uncomfortably aware of the pressure mounting inside him.

He gave a deep sigh, knowing that he was going to kiss Erin. The idea of being friends had sounded reasonable at the time, but as he felt her breasts molding tightly against his chest, he knew the folly of that suggestion. He placed his hands on her head and pulled her face from his neck gently. Their eyes met in defeated recognition of what was about to happen, for they both knew what they needed at this moment—the touch of each other's lips, the feel of each other's hands, the wondrous knowledge that they were both still very much alive.

"I'm going to kiss you, Erin Holmes. Don't be afraid," he whispered huskily. "I'm only going to kiss you."

75

She closed her eyes once more, her fingers running across the smoothness of his jaw, and nodded quietly. "I want that, Price. I want that very much."

"Open your eyes, Erin. I want you to see me kiss you. I want you to know how incredibly lovely you are; how it wouldn't matter to me if you weighed three hundred pounds or if you were Miss America at this moment. I want you to see that the Erin Holmes I'm kissing is going to make some lucky man a nearly perfect wife someday."

Her eyes opened slowly as his mouth brushed hers lightly.

"Do you believe that?" he whispered softly.

"I feel very lovely right now," she whispered against the pressure of his kiss. "You make me feel—very lovely. Thank you."

"Then close your eyes again, lovely Erin, because I'm going to kiss you in a way you'll never forget."

She moaned low in her throat as his mouth closed over hers, and his arms crushed her tighter to his chest, the kiss becoming hungry and urgent between them. His tongue prodded gently to enter her mouth and join with hers. His restless hands searched urgently down the sides of her breasts, stopping for just the barest moment to cup the swelling fullness, savoring the feel of her. He didn't want to scare her. He knew that most likely Quinn had led her into womanhood; but that was Quinn, not Price. He had promised her friendship, nothing more, and he would not break that promise. Right now she was very vulnerable, very lonely, very hurting. From her response to him right now as her mouth eagerly accepted his kiss, he knew he could ease their sexual agony of the last six months. But was that what he really wanted? Would that be fair to her, when he had no intention of it being anything but what it was—casual sex.

She moaned again, softly, like a small kitten, as his mouth left hers abruptly. He kissed her eyelids, her nose, her cheeks before burying his face in her hair one final time.

"I think we'd better break this up—unless you want it to go further," he said quietly. It would be her decision. He wanted her right now with a deep, aching need. But he also knew he would have to face her in the morning.

"I don't know . . . what I want," she whispered painfully. "I've never been with anyone but Quinn."

Price chuckled and brushed his lips across hers again. "You don't have to tell me that. But I know if you're feeling what I'm feeling, six months is a long time. . . ." His mouth took hers in another long, lazy kiss. "You say the word. I think we could bring each other a lot of pleasure tonight." He moved her closer against him to let her feel the powerful proof of his words.

Erin's thoughts were whirling. Price had awakened a hungry need in her, one that had lain dormant for a long time now. She had given herself in love to one man and felt very disillusioned from the experience. But at least she had loved him! With Price it would be wrong, because she didn't love him. She barely knew him.

With a beaten sigh she backed away from his arms, knowing that it had to mean something to her—she had to love a man before she could ever make another commitment that serious.

"I'm sorry, Price, but I'm not Jeannie, and you're not Quinn."

A startled look crossed Price's handsome features at her words. "Quinn! Were you thinking of *him*—that no good —you were thinking of him right now when I kissed you!" he said in an incredulous voice.

"Well, sort of. And don't tell me you weren't thinking of Jeannie!" she shot back irritably. She was quite sure all that pent-up passion hadn't been strictly for her.

"No, I wasn't!" He paused, a little surprised at his own answer. He really hadn't been thinking about Jeannie. For the first time in a very long time, he had kissed a woman other than Jeannie—and enjoyed it.

"You weren't?" Erin's eyes raised to meet his.

"No, I was not! And it sure doesn't do much for a man's ego to hear that the woman he's kissing is thinking about another man!"

"Well, what are you getting upset about? If I recall our earlier conversations, neither one of us is interested in anything other than friendship at the moment, and if we happen to want to exchange a friendly kiss—" Her face turned a soft shade of pink as she thought about their earlier "friendly" kiss. To her recollection, Quinn hadn't kissed her with such mastery even in the throes of passion!

"I may not be the most experienced man in the world, lady, but I would hardly consider what we just shared a friendly kiss! I'd bet my last dollar I could have—"

"You most certainly could not have!" Erin gasped indignantly. "Are you insinuating that I'm some sex-starved woman who can't wait to fall into bed with a man!"

"Keep your voice down!" Price cautioned heatedly. "You're going to wake the children up!"

"I want you to take back what you just said," Erin hissed angrily.

"About what?"

"About me being a sex-starved woman who can't wait to fall into a man's bed!"

"You're nuts! I didn't say that, you did!"

"Mr. Seaver!" Erin drew herself up fully and stared him boldly in the eye. "I believe we are going to have to reconsider the idea of being friends. My *friends* do not talk to me in the manner in which you just addressed me."

"Nuts. You are just plain nuts!" he shouted as he jumped up from the sofa. "From the minute I walked into this house, you have ranted and raved at me just because I happen to remind you of that scum—and you're right!

I do *not* think of you as a friend. You're a damn desirable woman—"

"Don't you *dare* call Quinn scum!"

"Good lord! Are you defending him now?"

"No, but you don't hear me saying anything derogatory about that—that—floozie you're in love with!"

"Let's just keep Jeannie's name out of this!"

"See!" Erin pointed her finger at him accusingly. "See! You even admit what she is. Why would you continue to be in love with a woman who dumped you for another man—probably not half as nice as you are. Why would you let a woman like that keep you from falling in love with someone else and having your five kids!"

"How did we get onto my problems? Why don't we discuss the possibility of you getting that no-good louse Quinn Daniels out of your system, lady! What reason have you got for still carrying a torch around for a man who isn't fit to wipe your shoes, let alone deserve your love. He'll never make any woman a decent husband! You just tell me that, Erin Holmes!"

"I don't have to tell you anything, Price Seaver, except I think you should leave—right now—tonight!"

"No, thank you. I'm on my vacation. Remember?" Price's face bore a very stubborn look now as he paced in front of Erin angrily.

She stood and faced him hostilely. "You *are* going to leave! Tonight!"

"No, no, I'm not." Price casually seated himself on the sofa again and picked up his glass. "Nathan is one of my best friends, and he would be offended if I stayed anywhere else. Besides, I'm doing him a favor. I'm sure he doesn't have the least idea that he's left his children in the hands of a dingbat who doesn't seem to have any control over them—"

"And you do?" she sputtered. "What about the green dog, the dead goldfish, the painted desert in the twins' bedroom—not to mention the demolished interior of your car . . ."

"I was getting ready to trade it in anyway." He dismissed her argument with a shrug. "Besides, I think they know who's boss now."

"Well, good, then you can take care of them. I'm going back home." Erin started toward her bedroom angrily.

"Hey! Now wait a minute—come back here." Price sprang to his feet. "We can work this out like two reasonable adults, can't we? I'm just going to hang around for a couple of days, get in some fishin', then I'll leave. I haven't had a vacation in years! You wouldn't do that to a friend, would you?" he pleaded helplessly.

"A friend, no; but we are not friends, Mr. Seaver. I should never have been so gullible as to believe that we could be," Erin said tightly.

"You're upset over that kiss, aren't you? I *told* you that I was going to kiss you, and if I remember right, your exact words were"—his voice grew high and feminine— " 'I'd like that.' But if it makes you feel any better, I'll keep my distance from you. That is, unless you signal me otherwise."

"Don't hold your breath," Erin said curtly. If she had any common sense, she would insist on him leaving tonight. But, on the other hand, it would be nice to have him around to help with the twins, and the next couple of days would be made considerably easier if he was around—and, if she would only admit it, she wanted him to stay. "All right, I'll confess I can use the help with the twins. But in two days you go home."

"Yes, ma'am," he agreed with a willing smile. "Are we semifriends again?"

"Barely," she acknowledged, the faint beginnings of a smile on her own face.

"I tell you what. Do you like fish?"

"Sure, why?"

"Well, in order to show you what a really nice guy I can be, I'll catch you a stringer of fish. Would you consent to fix them for me and the twins if I did?" His face had turned almost boyish as he tried to make amends.

"Just make it one big one and I'll consider it." She grinned.

"That's a deal, Erin." His face grew serious. "I really am sorry about a few minutes ago . . . I didn't mean to say those things about Quinn. It's none of my business how you feel about him."

"That's all right, Price. I shouldn't have said what I did about Jeannie. I know you must love her very much."

"I don't know if I do or not." The words surprised Price as well as Erin. A broad grin broke over his face. "At least right at the moment, I don't!"

"Good!" Erin grasped his hand sincerely. "You're much too nice a man to let a woman like her throw you."

"Well, I don't know about you, but I could use some sleep." Price stretched, then yawned. "How about taking the kids over to Silver Dollar City tomorrow?"

"You're not going to fish?"

"I'll get up and go early. I should be back by noon. Boy, I'd love to catch a trophy bass!" he said.

"I think that sounds like fun. I know the twins will be elated."

"Good. Then I guess I'll see you tomorrow." He walked across the room, turning out lamps as he went. Erin followed behind him, yawning. Bed would feel unusually good to her tonight.

The room was plunged into darkness, with only the faint light coming from the hallway. It seemed she was acutely aware of the broadness of his shoulders tonight, the very faint aroma of his aftershave, the way his hair looked so thick and touchable.

"Goodnight—friend," he whispered as they stopped before her bedroom door.

"Goodnight—friend," she whispered back, dreamily recalling the way his mouth had felt on hers, the warmth and moistness of it.

"You really are some woman," he said softly, his finger reaching out to brush away an errant lock of her hair. "Quinn Daniels is not only a rat, he's the world's biggest fool."

"No bigger than Jeannie."

"Jeannie who?" he asked, his smile growing tender.

"I'll see you tomorrow." She opened the door to her bedroom, not daring to stay in his presence a moment longer. He had awakened all those old feelings in her, and it made her very edgy.

"Yeah, see you tomorrow," Price said, his eyes lingering on the curve of her breast.

He was still leaning negligently against the doorjamb when she closed the door quietly. Jeannie who? Quinn who? At that moment Erin didn't really want to think about either one of them. At that moment neither one of them mattered. She was foolishly succumbing to Price Seaver's charms, and it suddenly scared her spitless!

CHAPTER FIVE

True to his word, Price was back shortly before noon the following day. The twins met him at the door, jabbering excitedly about their forthcoming trip to Silver Dollar City that afternoon.

"Just give me ten minutes for a quick shower, then we'll be on our way," he promised, trying to fight his way out of their clutches. He looked up and saw Erin standing in the doorway and gave her a sexy wink. "Hi, friend!"

"Hi! Any luck with the fish dinner?"

"Nope, didn't even catch a keeper this morning. The man who does a lot of guiding in this area is going out with me in the morning," he added hopefully.

"Hurry and take your shower, Uncle Pwice," Holly urged, taking his hand and pushing him toward the bathroom. "We're in an awful hurry!"

"We are, are we? Well, I'll see if I can't speed things up some," he promised her as she pushed him along.

The phone rang as Erin tried to smother a smile at the way Holly was manhandling him down the hallway, her mouth going nonstop.

"Hello," Erin said as she picked up the phone and sat down on the kitchen bar stool.

"Hello. May I speak to Price Seaver, please." A sultry voice floated over the wire. "His office said he could be reached at this number."

"Yes, he's here. Just a minute." Erin's stomach fluttered nervously as she laid the phone down and walked toward the bathroom. She couldn't imagine who was calling him, but an unreasonable surge of jealousy shot through her.

"Price, you're wanted on the phone. Are you able to take it?"

"Yo! I'll be there in a second."

Erin walked back to the phone and relayed the message. Within minutes Price walked into the room wearing only a pair of jeans. Erin forced herself to look at everything in the room but his bare, incredibly sexy chest.

"Yeah, Price Seaver here." The happy look of only moments earlier faded slowly from his face as he recognized the voice on the other end of the line. "Hello, Jeannie. How did you know I was here?" he said calmly.

A sudden feeling of nausea rose swiftly in Erin's throat as she tried to ignore the conversation. She busied herself with straightening up a few stray glasses from the kitchen counter.

"Well, I'm sorry to hear that. Maybe you two can still work things out." Price's voice remained very calm as his eyes glanced over and met Erin's.

Feeling very uncomfortable standing in the room while he was talking to Jeannie, Erin decided to see about the twins. She didn't want to hear the rest of the conversation. Apparently Jeannie's new love hadn't worked out.

It was at least another twenty minutes before Price finished his conversation, dressed, and returned to the living room. Erin was reading Huntley and Holly a story from one of their picture books, trying desperately to tell herself it didn't matter that he was talking to a woman he had loved—or still was very much in love with. It both puzzled and frightened her that she cared who he talked with. Had she jumped out of the frying pan into the fire?

"Sorry I took so long. Everybody ready to go?" Price greeted them absently. He looked over at Erin and smiled.

"We've been weady since we got up this morning," Holly grumbled, then jumped down from the sofa and wrapped her arms around Price's knee.

"Can we ride Fire in the Hole, Uncle Pwice?"

"What's a fire in the hole?" He grimaced, trying to undo her prying fingers.

"A roller coaster!" Huntley filled him in. "But I don't know if we're tall enough to ride it yet. We'll have to measure again today. You have to be th-is tall," he stretched his hands over his head as far as he could reach.

"Well, I'll make it, but I don't know about you two munchkins." He glanced at Erin. "You ready to go, Auntie Erin?"

"Yes, all ready." Every nerve in her was screaming to ask him what Jeannie had wanted, but she knew she was being completely unreasonable. It was really none of her business. They all trooped out to the front door, the twins' enthusiasm bubbling over.

"Lord, I wish I had half the energy those kids have," Price complained as he locked the front door. "If a person could bottle that, he would be a millionaire!"

"Why don't we take my car," Erin suggested as they walked down the steps. "I hate to do any more damage to yours, and they certainly can't hurt mine."

They stopped in front of her red Volkswagen and stared at the little bug. "It isn't running right, but I think it will get us over there and back," she added.

"Sure, why not. Come on, kids, get in Aunt Erin's crackerbox."

"Kwackerbox!" Holly's eyes lit up. "Is this weally a kwackerbox!"

"No, of course not. That's just your uncle Price's idea of a joke. This is a very nice, *cheap* car. Not all of us can afford a luxurious car like his." She looked at Price pointedly.

Price got in on the driver's side and started the engine.

"I'll tell you what. I'll give you the Olds when Santa Claus brings me my lellow Maserati."

"And your bird slippers," Huntley added helpfully.

"And my bird slippers," Price agreed. "I plan on wearing those everywhere I go."

It took a little over twenty minutes to drive to the amusement park. The lush Ozarks countryside was still thick with green foliage, but in another month the hills would be ablaze with the beauty of fall.

Price wheeled the small car into one of the large parking lots and they all got out, the twins barely able to control their excitement.

"Don't walk too far ahead of us," Erin called as the twins spurted forward, eager to get into the park where everything was set in the frontier days of the 1800s.

"They'll be all right. Let them work off some of that energy." Price laughed as they walked toward the tram that would take them to the entrance of the city. "Aren't you going to ask me about that phone call earlier?" he asked as he reached out and took her hand.

"It's none of my business," Erin replied, her stomach fluttering wildly at his touch.

"No, but I thought that since we were friends, you'd naturally wonder why Jeannie was calling."

They walked together in silence for a minute before Erin's curiosity overcame her. "What did she want?"

Price looked down at her and asked innocently, "Who?"

"Price!"

"Oh, you mean ole what's her name . . . Jeannie."

"Yes, ole what's her name. What did she want?"

"Well, it seems her newfound love has not worked out the way she expected."

"And she wants you back," Erin finished.

"She didn't say."

"What *did* she say?"

86

"Not a whole lot of anything, actually. I think she just wanted someone to air her gripes to, someone to feel sorry for her."

"And you obliged."

"I listened. I didn't necessarily agree with all she said."

"You would be an utter fool to take her back, Price. And mark my words, that's what she wants," Erin said bluntly, fighting that ridiculous feeling of jealousy again.

"Do tell, Auntie Erin. By the way, I've been meaning to ask you why the twins call you aunt."

"I don't know. They have always called me Aunt Erin from the moment they learned how to talk. What about you? You're not their uncle."

"Brenda started calling me that in front of them, and they just picked up on it. I don't mind; I enjoy it," he confessed. "But back to why I shouldn't go back to Jeannie. You were saying. . . ."

"I didn't say you shouldn't go back to her. I just said *I* thought you would be foolish to, that's all."

They walked together, Price holding her hand, both of them deep in thought. Finally Price broke the silence. "I'm flying up to Memphis tomorrow. I called my office after I hung up with Jeannie, and there's a matter that has to be taken care of. I should be back home in time for dinner."

Erin's heart sank. He was going to Memphis to see Jeannie, and he was using work as an excuse.

"I can't get a plane out until around ten in the morning. I think I'll still try to keep that fishing date with John."

"John?"

"The fishing guide. I'd sure love to get me a trophy bass while I'm down here."

Erin barely heard his words as her mind rebelled against the fact that he would soon be back in that—that woman's arms. He was such a nice guy! He deserved more than

Jeannie would ever be able to give him. Why were men such blind fools when it came to women.

The tram pulled up to the station, and they all boarded. The afternoon was perfect for an outing. The fierce heat of the summer had eased somewhat, making the day a little more comfortable for the foursome.

"When God made Missouri, he sure knew what he was doin'," Price remarked as his eyes took in the majestic hills and valleys around them. "A man would have to go a long way ever to find the beauty that's spread out here before us."

"It is beautiful," Erin agreed, pleased that he still held her hand.

The tram deposited them at the entrance gate, and Price paid their way in. For the next few hours they were visitors in the Old West, in an era when things happened at a much slower pace. A rugged sheriff met them as they entered the city and deputized the twins, much to their giggling delight. Everywhere they looked there was some type of food to tempt even the most dedicated dieter. Funnel cakes, delicious batter fried in deep fat, then sprinkled with powdered sugar; fresh pies; strawberries and ice cream; barbequed chicken; corn on the cob; gigantic hot chocolate chip cookies; homemade candies—the smells and the selections went on and on. Handmade crafts abounded and, of course, the rides that all children looked forward to.

They had just gone on The Great American Plunge, a log ride that boasted a five-story drop at the end of it, and emerged laughing and dripping wet. Erin's stomach was threatening to rid itself of the ice cream she had eaten prior to the ride.

"Let's go on Fire in the Hole, Uncle Price," Huntley urged, undaunted by the hair-raising ride they had just taken.

"Oh, come on, Huntley, ole pal, have a heart!" Price groaned, pulling his wet shirt away from his chest.

"You pwomised," Holly fretted, wrapping herself around his leg again.

"You know, you've got a bad habit of doing that, squirt. When you get older you're going to have to watch yourself. Some man's going to take offense when you wrap yourself around his leg like that," he said teasingly, pulling a lock of her hair playfully and winking at Erin knowingly.

"Oh, Uncle Pwice, you're siwwy." Holly giggled. "Can we wide Fire in the Hole?"

Price looked at Erin pleadingly and said, "Do we have to, Aunt Erin?"

"We better go measure and see if you're tall enough," she warned with a grin.

"Oh, brother," Price grumbled. "I haven't got a prayer. I *know* I'm tall enough!"

Price's face was almost comically relieved a few minutes later when the twins failed to make the mark by half an inch.

"Oh, dawn it," Holly complained. "I don't think I'll ever get that big." Her eyes surveyed the marker hostilely.

"Yes, you will. Next year you'll be able to ride nearly everything in the park," Erin assured her.

"Let's do something sane and logical like having our picture taken," Price suggested, scooping Holly up in his arms and nuzzling her neck with his hair. Erin was amazed at how well he handled the twins. He rarely seemed to lose his patience with them.

They wandered over to the tintype picture section, and each one selected a costume to wear. When the photographer sat them down, they looked like a typical young pioneer family. Price and Huntley wore coonskin hats and carried black-powder muzzle loaders. Erin and Holly

89

were decked out prettily in sun bonnets and long cotton dresses.

"Now, Mommy and Daddy, you hold the children between you and group in real close together," the photographer instructed Price and Erin.

Price grinned at Erin and reached for one of the twins. "You get the other one, Mommy."

Erin felt a surge of pride for one brief moment as the real world faded away and she was indeed holding her and Price's child on her lap as the picture was taken.

Since it was going to be awhile before the picture would be developed, they decided to take a ride in the flooded mine. As they boarded the boats to ride through the cool, dark cave, Price sat Huntley and Holly in the seat in front of them. "We can keep a better eye on them this way," he explained with a devilish twinkle in his eye. Before they had each taken a twin and sat with them on a ride. "Besides, I'll probably have to protect you in that dark cave," he whispered for her benefit alone.

"I've always made out all right before." Erin grinned saucily. "Nothing's ever attacked me yet."

"Ah, then you haven't been riding with the right person." He grinned back. "Maybe your luck will change."

For once the twins sat perfectly still, never moving a muscle as the floating ride entered the dark, cool interior of the cave. The passing scenery and loud music held their complete attention, making them oblivious to everything else.

Erin was aware of Price's arms slipping around her long before he pulled her closer to him and whispered huskily in her ear, "I've been waiting all day for you to send me some sort of signal." His warm breath sent shivers racing up and down her spine.

"Signal—concerning what?" Erin pretended innocence, loving the way his arms tightened around her possessively.

"Oh, we're going to play hard to get, are we," he murmured, nuzzling her neck. "All right, I'll come right out with it. I've been going crazy all day wanting to kiss you. How about getting me out of my misery?" His mouth worked warmly along the column of her creamy neck.

"You're missing the best part of the ride," she protested weakly as her body came alive under the touch of his lips. "It's dark and scary."

"Why do you think I picked this particular ride? I'm no dummy. Besides, I've already seen all of it anyway."

The feel of his fingers gently stroking the bare flesh on her arms sent her senses reeling. She leaned her head against the comfort of his shoulder, remembering how he had looked with just his jeans on. She could almost feel the softness of that thick dark hair that stretched across the span of his broad chest.

"Um . . . what kind of perfume do you use? You always smell so good," he murmured against her hair. "Even after a day like we've put in today, you smell all fresh and clean." One large hand gently caressed the silkiness of her arm. "Forgive me, but I can't help wondering what you would feel like lying beside me in my arms at night—what it would feel like to be able to reach out and touch all those soft womanly curves . . ."

"Price, please. I don't think you should be talking this way."

"I'm not suggesting we do all those things. I was just wondering out loud," he defended meekly, his lips finding their way to her ear, taking the white lobe between his strong teeth and biting playfully. "You'd probably be real upset if I told you what I was thinking about awhile ago when you bent over to tie Holly's shoe."

"Price!"

"Oh, I know, I'm fresh, aren't I?" His tongue reached out and touched her ear now as his hand slipped around her rib cage to cup one soft breast. "But I won't tell anyone if you don't."

91

"I'm glad it's pitch dark in here," Erin whispered against his ear now. "We would be making a complete spectacle of ourselves."

"We? I don't see you doing anything—" His words were cut off by her mouth closing over his. For the next few minutes they exchanged long, languid kisses, their breathing becoming deeper, the kisses becoming more hungry and intense. Erin seemed to fit perfectly in his arms, and his hands tenderly explored her body, pulling her tight against him, letting her feel and exult in the effect she was having on him in their own private, dark world. In his arms she felt like a new, totally desirable woman.

Hesitantly she unbuttoned the first button of his shirt and let her hand run gently over his chest. The touch of his skin on her fingertips brought a whole new surge of longing to her. She had tasted the delights between man and woman, and her body was now crying out to be loved again.

"Erin," he whispered huskily, his mouth finding hers hotly, their tongues merging in a frenzy of ravishing kisses.

"Uncle Pwice! Wook." Holly's voice broke into their thoughts, each one forgetting where they were for the moment. "Wook at that thing!" She pointed a chubby finger at some of the passing scenery. Erin could see the light at the end of the ride and knew that they would be coming out of the cave very soon now.

"I see it, Holly." Price's voice sounded shaky as he reluctantly released Erin and buttoned his shirt. He leaned over and gave her one quick kiss. "That was one hell of a signal, lady," he said with a grin.

As their little boat shot out into the sunlight, Erin blinked at the brightness of the day. Her mind was still back in the cave and on the way she had responded to Price's kisses. What was the matter with her? Could she have fallen in love so quickly, so unexpectedly? Would she be so foolish as to lay herself wide open for new heartache and disappointment? She and Price could never make it. He was not her perfect man. He was still in love with another woman or, at best, certainly unwilling to step into another love affair so soon after the last disastrous one. He had as many hangups about love and marriage as she did at the moment.

"You've gotten awfully quiet," Price said as they walked through the park, letting the twins run toward the zoo. "Anything wrong?"

Erin smiled and reached for his hand as they walked. "No, just thinking."

"About anything in particular?"

"No, nothing."

"Do you think you could ever forget Quinn, Erin? I mean really forget him," Price asked quietly as they stopped and sat on a bench in front of the children's zoo.

Erin leaned back and looked at the cloudless blue sky, her mind trying to see Quinn's face. For some reason it wouldn't appear. Even more strange, she realized she didn't want it to.

"I spend most of my time trying to forget him. I think one of these days I might make it. Quinn was the first man I ever fell in love with, the first and only man that I . . . Well, it's just that I don't take things like that lightly. I thought I'd probably spend the rest of my life with him, and when that didn't happen, it hurt me a great deal. I don't ever want to leave myself open to that type of hurt again."

"But you do want to marry sometime in the future?" Price asked softly.

"I thought I did, but you're right: There is no perfect marriage, no perfect man. I think I'll spend the next few years just getting to know myself and what I really want out of life. Who knows—I may be cut out to be an old maid." She laughed. "If you're a bachelor and I'm an old

93

maid, we'd make a fine pair of friends, wouldn't we? We could just sit back and be an aunt and uncle to all our friends' children and content ourselves with that—" Her voice broke off in a sob.

"I doubt that it will come to that," Price assured her. "I have a feeling you're destined for motherhood, the perfect marriage, the whole nine yards. You're just going to have to be a little patient, wait until your knight in shining armor can find you."

"If you want my true opinion, I think his horse threw him somewhere in the forest." She grinned despite her misty eyes.

"Naw, I don't think so," Price scoffed. "He'll come ridin' up someday, sweep you off your feet . . . that is, if you manage to get that ten pounds off. . . ."

"Price Seaver! You cad!"

"Come on. Let's go find the kids and eat." He laughed, dodging her punch.

"Again? You surely couldn't be hungry!" It seemed they had done nothing but eat since they entered the park.

"Starved. I'm not the one trying to lose weight. Come on, chubby, let's eat in the old mine." He grabbed her hand and pulled her toward the petting pen. "If you're good, I'll let you pet one of these stinkin' goats!"

"You're spoiling me, Price." She made a face at him. He made one back.

"For someone who couldn't eat a bite, you did a terrific job of it on all that fried chicken," Price teased an hour later as they emerged from "dining in the mine."

"Yes, but I really didn't think I was going to get that last piece of pie down," she reminded him sternly. "I told you I didn't want it."

"Sure, you didn't," he agreed, winking at Huntley and Holly. "If I hadn't bought you that piece of pie, you would

94

have created a scene, and disgraced both the twins and me. Now admit it, chubby."

"It was good." She grinned. "Even if I did add another five pounds."

Price stood back and surveyed her curves critically. "Wherever it went, it looks good." His eyes met hers boldly. "Real good."

"Let's go get our picture, Uncle Price," Huntley said, beginning to show the first signs of slowing down.

"That's a great idea, Huntley," Erin agreed. "Let's get the picture and go home. I'm exhausted."

Fifteen minutes later they were giggling together over the picture of the very stern-looking pioneer family who stared back at them from the tintype picture.

"We look like we lost our last friend on earth," Price said with a chuckle. "Look how solemn ole Huntley looks."

They broke out in peals of laughter again as they surveyed the solemn look on the little boy's face.

"That man *said* to look serious," Huntley protested, beginning to get a bit put out at their continued laughter. It was one thing to laugh with someone and quite another to be laughed at.

"I want some popcorn," Holly yelled above the laughter.

"Oh, Holly! Surely not!" Erin collapsed against Price in another round of laughter. His strong arms caught her to him and held her tightly for a moment. Her laughter faded as their eyes met. She suddenly had the uncontrollable desire to reach out and kiss him. From the look in his eyes, he would have no objections; on the contrary, he would encourage it.

"Here, Huntley, you take the money and take your sister to that cart over there and buy her some popcorn. Think you can handle that?"

"Sure, Uncle Price, I'm big now." Huntley beamed at the rare opportunity to assert his masculinity.

"Hold Holly's hand," Erin called as they skipped happily away. "Do you think we should let them go alone?" she asked worriedly.

"Good grief, they'll never be out of our eyesight, worrywart!"

"I know, but they're still such babies." Erin sighed.

"Who do you think should get custody of this picture?" Price asked, turning their thoughts back to the tintype he was holding. "I suppose we should let Brenda and Nathan have it."

Erin peered over his shoulder at the photograph, a feeling of sadness coming over her. Today had been one of the most fun-filled days of her life. Being with Price had made her forget all the bad times she had experienced during the last few months. For the first time in a long time, she had laughed—really laughed. The day was drawing to an end, and she desperately wished she could make it last forever.

"We should have bought more than one," she said softly. She hated to let him know it, but she wanted that picture.

"Do you want it?" Price asked, glancing up at her.

"Oh, I don't know . . ." she hedged courteously.

"If you don't, I do." Price didn't hedge for a moment. "You sure you don't mind?"

What could she say? She should have spoken up. "No, I don't mind, but what could an old bachelor like you want with a picture like that?" she asked teasingly.

"He'll probably sit and drool over the old maid who's in it."

Erin's eyes dropped shyly. "Oh, Price. . . ."

"I got it, Uncle Price. I got the popcorn!" Huntley came dragging Holly back with him, trailing popcorn for several yards.

Price peered into the almost-empty box. "I think you spilled some, pal."

"I want some ice cream," Holly whined against the side of Erin's jeans.

"I don't think you know what you want," Erin said, hugging her little body close. "I think we'd better all go home before we bankrupt Uncle Price."

They left the park, a tired but happy group. Price slipped his arm around Erin and she leaned on his shoulder tiredly as they walked back to the car.

"It's been a beautiful day, Price. Thank you," she murmured as the twins ran happily ahead of them.

"I should be thanking you," he protested in a contented voice. "I can't remember when I've spent a more enjoyable day."

"I wish you didn't have to go tomorrow," she added, foolishly hoping he would forget that a woman named Jeannie had ever existed.

"I wish I didn't have to also," he replied simply. "But I'll be back."

Their eyes met each other's briefly before Erin turned away. She was overcome with the almost childish urge to make him promise—promise that he would come back. But what if he didn't come back? What if, when he saw Jeannie, all those old feelings of love resurfaced and he took her back? And if he did come back? What then? Was she even remotely close to committing herself to another man—committing her love, her very fragile feelings, her very tender and bruised heart to this tall man walking beside her.

At the moment there was only one thing Erin was sure of, one thing that would never change on her list of priorities. Before anything could ever seriously develop between her and Price, she would have to know that Jeannie was totally out of his life and his thoughts. She laughed ironically to herself. What gave her the idea Price would ever consider anything serious between them? He had been hurt just as deeply as she had been. Although they had had a wonderful time together today, could it be that he *did* think of her as only a friend? Maybe he was only letting down his reserve for a brief time while he took a few days off from work, a few days away from his own problems. Questions, questions, and for Erin, no answers.

She shook herself mentally. What was the matter with her! People didn't fall in love with each other in two days.

That thought was comforting and helped boost her sagging spirits considerably.

As they drove along the quiet countryside, dusk was just beginning to settle over the lake area. Holly sat on Erin's lap while Huntley hung over Price's seat and chattered nonstop about his pet frog, Roscoe P. Coltrane.

The little red car pulled into the Daniels' drive, and at least two of the occupants exited rowdily.

Price gave Erin a deprecatory grin. "I think I'm getting old."

"Me, too." She yawned. "I think we're both ready for a shower and something cold to drink."

Price opened the car door and got out. "Boy, that sounds great! I'll get Cathy next door to watch the kids for us."

"Watch the kids. Whatever for?" Erin paused and looked at him in surprise.

"So we can take *our* shower," Price replied with a wicked grin.

"Price," Erin gave him a tolerant smile, "*we* are not going to take a shower. *I* am."

Price's face fell. "I thought your words were too good to be true."

"Uncle Pwice, can I catch some lighties?" Holly ran over and grabbed him around the leg and hung on as he tried to walk to the house.

"I don't know, puddin'. What's a lightie?"

"Dem bugs." She pointed a pudgy finger at the fireflies swirling in the gathering twilight.

"I think dem bugs would prefer their freedom, squirt." Price gave her a hug and a gentle swat on her bottom. "Let's get you cleaned up and ready for bed."

Amid violent protests Erin and Price finally had the twins in their pajamas. A round of kisses, pleas for drinks of water, trips to the bathroom and unusually long prayers delayed their arrival in bed yet another twenty minutes.

At last, with a sigh of relief, Erin turned off the bedroom light and left two five-year-olds sleeping peacefully. Price draped his arm casually around her waist as they walked down the hallway. "You hungry?"

Erin shook her head in amusement. "No, I'm not hungry. Surprised?"

"Floored." Price smiled at her tenderly.

"I'm just tired. Being a mother is the most exhausting job in the world. You never get a day off!"

"You're a darn good mother. Did you know that?"

Erin laid her head on his shoulder as they ambled toward the living room. "Thank you. You're not bad as a father, either. Your five unborn kids don't know what they're missing," she teased.

They strolled into the living room, their eyes catching a brief view of the lake through the moon-drenched window.

"It's beautiful out there tonight. Warm enough for a swim." Price glanced at her suggestively. "If you don't want to take a shower together, how about going for a swim with me? I promise I'll behave."

"Sure you would." Erin turned away from him and sat down on the sofa.

"I would!" Price defended. "Come on, Auntie Ewin. The twins are sound asleep, and we could hear them if they woke up. The lake's practically at our back door."

"You're serious," she said with a laugh. "You really want to go out there and swim at this hour?"

Price consulted his watch. "It's not even ten o'clock."

"But we don't have any bathing suits. . . ."

"I know where Nathan and Brenda keep theirs, if you insist on using the burdensome things."

"Well, I certainly *do* insist on using them!"

Price was dragging her along behind him now. "Oh, good. Then you agree to go with me. You had me worried there for a minute, troll. I thought you'd try to tell me you looked like a blimp in your bathing suit."

"A blimp! I do not!" she protested heatedly as he stopped before Nathan and Brenda's bedroom door. "Maybe a little. . . ."

"Curvy. Curvy's the word you're looking for," Price supplied helpfully.

"Right! Curvy." Erin grinned. "*Real* curvy."

Price winked at her in a most sexy manner. "I can hardly wait to see all those curves stuffed into Brenda's bathing suit. Third drawer on the left."

"Do you promise you'll behave?" she asked with a groan as he pushed her through the door, then closed it.

"Of course," he answered dutifully, but for some reason Erin noticed his voice didn't ring true.

Erin was still grumbling ten minutes later as she made her way down the moonlit path wearing one of Brenda's outrageously skimpy bathing suits and a heavy terry cloth robe. Thank heavens it was dark and he couldn't get a good look at her attire, or what there was of it. Brenda had always been much more daring in her dress than Erin, and this string bikini emphasized the difference dramatically.

"Let's not get very far from the house," she cautioned, trying to keep up with his long-legged strides.

"We have to go far enough to reach the water," he

reasoned, catching her arm as she stumbled. "You're not only homely, you're clumsy, too, aren't you?"

"You're going to be missing some teeth, Mr. Seaver, the next time you refer to my looks," Erin warned grimly.

"Hey." Price turned around and smiled at her innocently. "*I* think you're real foxy. You're the one who keeps telling me you look like a slug."

"Some friend you are," Erin grumbled, marching behind him. "Why don't you try to humor me? Why don't you tell me how you don't think I look that bad! Maybe even outright lie to me and tell me you like fat girls!"

"I have told you that," Price said patiently, letting a tree limb slap back in her face carelessly, "but you won't believe me. Besides, I'm getting tired of this friend idea. I think I'd rather be 'lover' now," he said and grinned.

"Think again," she said curtly as they reached their destination.

Price peeled off the shirt he was wearing and reached for the button on his jeans.

"I hope you've got something on under there," Erin said, turning her face away in embarrassment.

"Am I supposed to? Gee, I'm sorry. Nathan's suits were all too big for me."

Erin clenched her teeth. "You had *better* be teasing."

"I never tease. Take a look."

"No."

"Aw, come on. Haven't you ever gone skinny-dippin'?"

"No—not with a—man." Erin was becoming nervous. Price was such a tease, she didn't know whether to take him seriously, but she was beginning to fear that for once he might be telling her the truth.

"Well," he said hastily, "I'm offering you one last chance to feast your eyes—then I'm going in."

"Don't let me keep you," Erin said tightly. Surely he was kidding!

"Aren't you going to take your robe off and join me?"

"Yes. Turn your head."

"Why? Are you going to surprise me? It's too much to hope for, isn't it, that underneath all that serious little bundle of sexy curves, there could lurk a jaded, evil woman who's going to make a man out of me."

Erin jerked the robe off, keeping her eyes anxiously averted from him. "Make a man out of you? I'm sure I'm fifteen years too late for that."

"Let's see, I'm thirty-three, so fifteen years ago I would have been eighteen . . . umm, gad! You're uncanny! How did you know? Did you know Boom-Boom Taggert?"

"No! I did not know Boom-Boom Taggert!" Erin whirled angrily at his malicious taunting, "but I gather you did!"

Price's smile vanished as he let out a low, admiring whistle. The moon shone on Erin's curvaceous body, the black string bikini revealing how truly lovely Price's little troll actually was. "Good grief, Erin, I knew you were a doll, but I must admit I never thought you'd look this good. . . ." His voice trailed off huskily as his eyes roamed over her intimately.

"Does—does it look all right?" she asked shyly, meeting his gaze in the moonlight.

"It looks fine." His eyes seemed to be devouring her now.

For the first time Erin noticed that he did have brief swimming trunks on. She couldn't make out the color, but at the moment, who cared? All she could see was the broad expanse of his chest, the way his stomach lay flat and smooth, the hard muscles of his legs.

"Then will you stop teasing me about being—a troll?"

"Probably not, but when I do, you'll know I'm only teasing you." His voice was affectionate as he reached out and gently touched her face. "Come here, troll, and kiss me."

He moved forward to take her in his arms as she ducked and stepped past him.

"You said you would behave," she reminded with a giggle. Her heart was pounding loudly in her chest, and she felt slightly breathless. There would undoubtedly be trouble if they both stood here in the moonlight and took notes on each other's bathing suits!

"Oh, so you're one of *those* kind of women!" Price reached out and scooped her up in his arms, running toward the water with her.

"No, Price!" Erin hung on for dear life as they hit the cool water with a loud splash. The shock of the cold water took her breath away as they went under, then came back up sputtering. "That was cruel!" Erin gasped, wrapping her arms tighter around his neck.

"I know. I'm a real devil! Gosh you feel good." His hands ran along her rib cage exploringly.

Erin reached down and removed his roaming fingers. "You promised to behave."

"I'm *always* making promises and not being able to keep them." Price put his hands back where they had been.

"Quinn! Stop it," Erin pleaded, pushing him away.

Price's hands fell away immediately, his face growing solemn. "I'm not Quinn, Erin," he said quietly.

Erin realized her mistake at once. She didn't know how Quinn's name had slipped out.

"I know that, Price. I'm sorry. I don't even know why I said it," she apologized sincerely.

"Could it be because I remind you of him? That you still think of him constantly?" Price's voice had a tinge of sarcasm in it.

"No," Erin replied calmly, "I don't really think of him that often anymore. And as far as you reminding me of him . . ." Erin paused and cocked her head teasingly, her hands creeping back around his neck. "You don't remind me of him at all anymore. I knew you weren't a Quinn Daniels days ago."

"Oh. In what way am I *not* a Quinn Daniels?" His arms pulled her closer to him, their wet bodies meeting and clinging to each other comfortably. "I like a pretty woman as well as he does."

"You seem able to control yourself a little better." Erin's pulse skipped a beat at the feel of his solid male length against her.

"Control myself, huh?" He shifted her tighter against his mounting desire. "You call that control?"

"Price, remember, we're only friends." Erin flipped water in his face with one finger. "Too bad, huh?"

"Well, what I had in mind was very friendly," he defended, flipping water back.

"Don't get my hair wet."

"Are you serious? You look like a drowned rat!"

"There you go talking about my looks again! I suppose you never saw Jeannie with her hair wet."

Price's arms fell away from her sides as he pushed off into the dark water and swam for a few minutes, completely ignoring Erin's taunt. Erin swam toward him, feeling uneasy about being left alone in the dark water. Although the moon lit up the night, it was still a little eerie swimming in the lake at this hour. The only sounds came from the large bullfrogs croaking along the deserted shores.

She had only swum a few laps when she paused and looked hurriedly around for him. "Price? Where are you?"

The gentle lapping of the waves upon the shore was the only voice that answered her.

"Come on, Price! Answer me! I know you're there!"

Erin swam a little further out. She was becoming more uneasy by the moment. Where had he disappeared to? He had seemed like a strong swimmer. She peered ahead of her in the darkness, swallowing an urge to let out a loud, terrified scream.

Another couple of minutes went by before the scream materialized as she felt something latch onto her foot and drag her slowly beneath the water. Grasping wildly for something to hold onto, her hands came in contact with a pair of strong arms pulling her closely against a solid chest.

As they surfaced together, Price's mouth closed over hers hungrily. Although she could barely breathe, the touch of his lips was a delicious, heady sensation. His moist, firm mouth demanded a response and she freely gave it to him. He moved his mouth over hers, devouring its softness, molding her curves to the contours of his lean body. She didn't protest as his hands sought the snap on the top of her bathing suit and slowly let the scrap of fabric float away in the quiet water. His hand roamed intimately over her breast, sending cold shivers down her spine at the cool brush of his fingers on her skin.

"Don't," she managed to whisper weakly as their mouths finally broke apart.

"Why not?" he whispered back huskily. "You know I want you. Why do you keep fighting it?" His voice was filled with a curious deep longing as his mouth explored the hollow of her slender neck.

"Because . . . I don't think you're ready for this yet," she stammered helplessly as his lips moved down her shoulder sensuously. She couldn't help thinking about his trip tomorrow and the possibility that he would be seeing Jeannie. After tonight Erin might never see Price Seaver again, and although she wanted him in a way that was almost painful, she had to remember that another woman held his heart.

"I'm not?" Price drew her closer. "I know it's been a long time, but I'm nearly positive that I'm ready." He chuckled intimately.

"Oh, no, I didn't mean—" Erin broke off, embarrassed. There was certainly no doubt that he was ready. "I meant I don't think we should become this involved—this soon."

"Let me guess." Price sighed and buried his face in her neck defeatedly. "Quinn and Jeannie."

Only Jeannie, she wanted to say but didn't. Let him think she still loved Quinn. It would be easier this way. "Yes. Quinn and Jeannie," she agreed sadly.

"You know something? Right now I wish I'd never heard those two names," Price whispered tenderly against her ear. "Do you think there'll ever be a day when you get that damn man out of your system?"

"I don't know. Maybe. What about you and Jeannie?"

"What about me and Jeannie, what about me and Jeannie—you're worse than a damn cockatoo, Erin," Price said irritably. "What about me and Jeannie? We broke up over six months ago, woman! What else can I tell you?"

"You could tell me you don't love her anymore!" Erin shot back angrily.

"You could tell me the same thing about Quinn, but I don't hear you chattering nonstop about that."

"I do not chatter! And besides, why should I say that about Quinn?" Erin tossed her head haughtily.

"For the same reason I'm not going to say that about Jeannie. It's neither one of our business!" Price said just as haughtily.

"It should be!" Erin couldn't let it drop. "We're friends, remember!"

"Forget that crap! I don't want to be your friend," he said bluntly.

"You said you did!" Erin glared at him hostilely. "What have I done?"

"Nothing!" Price grumbled. "It was just a stupid idea. I've decided to stick to friends who aren't built like a brick—outhouse."

"You're holding that against me!"

Price looked longingly at her bare breasts in the soft moonlight. "I would be if you didn't talk so much."

"*I* do *not* talk so much! Basically I'm a very quiet, calm, level-headed person. *You're* the one who makes me a little crazy!" She sniffed disdainfully. This was one friendship she was glad to be rid of. "Kindly hand me my bathing-suit top."

"I can't."

"Why?"

"Because it's probably five miles down the lake by now."

"Then go get it!"

"No." He lay back and floated peacefully in the water. "If we were still friends, I'd think about it . . . But since we're not. . . ."

"You are making me angry, Price," Erin warned in a calm voice.

Price bobbled along happily, ignoring her temper.

Erin swam up to him and leaned down close. "I *said* you're making me *very angry,* Price. We are not going to be friends much longer unless you go get my bathing-suit top."

Price shrugged his shoulders. "I have found," he began in a philosophical tone, "that friends come and go. It's the enemies who seem to mount up. . . ." His voice began to gurgle as Erin slowly pushed his head under the water. As he was sputtering in amazement, she dove beneath him and with one angry jerk rid him of his bathing suit.

"What do you think you're doing?" he gasped indignantly.

"If you think I'm walking back up that hill half nude, then you're all wet—in more ways than one!" She scrambled hurriedly toward the bank.

He was still yelling threateningly at her as she made her way back up the moonlit path, his trunks clutched victoriously to her bare chest.

"Hey, Holmes!" he hollered. "I've changed my mind. Let's be friends again. How about it?"

"Fine with me, Seaver! Just as soon as you answer one lousy question!" she called back over her shoulder as she struggled up the vine-covered path.

"Wait a minute!" He stood up in the water, the moon glistening on his bare bottom. "What's the question?" He placed his hands on his hips arrogantly. "Don't tell me! Let me guess!"

Erin turned and her eyes met his in amusement for a moment. Then in one voice they both shouted simultaneously, *"What about Jeannie?"*

CHAPTER SIX

"Huntley, are you sure?"

Immense brown eyes peered back at Erin seriously. "I'm sure, Aunt Erin."

Disappointment flashed across Erin's face as she realized that she had missed Price this morning. She had wanted to see him, if only for a few minutes, before he left for Memphis.

"He's coming back tonight, isn't he?" Cathy asked as she poured a second cup of coffee for Erin.

"Yes, but I sort of wanted to talk to him before he left." She was sorry now that she had let the twins talk her into coming over to their nearest neighbor's house to play with a friend their own age.

"He put a bi-ig fish in the fwigewator," Holly lisped.

"Yeah, re-eally big!" Huntley agreed.

Erin smiled. Price must have caught a fish for their dinner this evening. She had laid out a roast this morning, but she could always use it for tomorrow's dinner. Stirring her coffee thoughtfully, she issued a silent prayer that he would be back to eat his fish dinner—that nothing—and no one—would delay his return.

"Don't forget the party tonight," Cathy was saying as she cut another slice of coffee cake and put it down in front of Erin.

"Oh, no, please. . . ." Erin pushed the plate away. "I've already eaten more than I should!"

"Are you sure?" Cathy mumbled between mouthfuls of the luscious, rich cinnamon cake.

"Positive." Erin had to be firm. She was going to get this extra weight off if it killed her. Jeannie was probably as slim as a reed, and if Erin had any hopes of competing with her—good heavens, there she went again! She wasn't going to eat another piece of coffee cake because she wanted to lose weight for herself! No one else. She was a strong, self-controlled person, and if she put her mind to it she could have ten pounds off in nothing flat. Her spirits soared as she imagined herself looking gaunt and willowy. Giving up that extra piece of cake was a snap.

"Send them over around five. I'm going to fix hot dogs before I take them to the carnival rides," Cathy added as the twins and her son Michael ran out the back door squealing like a bunch of hooligans.

"You are undoubtedly the bravest person alive." Erin laughed. For some reason she couldn't get her eyes off that darn piece of delicious, mouth-watering coffee cake. The bakery must have someone with a vicious streak to put out a dessert that looked and tasted like this!

"Thankfully, Trev will be here to help me with them. Taking six five-year-olds for the evening is not exactly my idea of fun!"

"It's very nice of you. I'm sure they'll have a wonderful time. I suppose I'll fix the fish Price caught this morning for our dinner. I have been worrying about letting the twins eat any because of the bones, so this would be a good time to get it over with." Her hand reached out and unconsciously picked up the plate of cake. "If he caught a big enough one, I'll send you and Trevor over a plateful," she offered as she forked the yummy cake into her mouth hungrily.

"That would be great. Trev loves fresh fish."

"Well, if the fish is as big as the twins say, I'll have enough to feed an army," she mused between forkfuls.

"Darn! I wish they had come in and told me Price was back from fishing!"

"You know those kids. They were too busy playing to think of anything else. Price probably called them over and showed them the fish, and their little minds dismissed it as soon as they ran out of the house again."

"I'm sure he was in a hurry," Erin reasoned as she stuck the last bite of cake into her mouth. "He had to catch a plane around ten." She glanced down at the empty plate before her. "Good grief! I ate that cake!"

Cathy peered at the barren china. "You nearly ate the dish!"

"Oh, brother," Erin moaned, shoving the plate away in disgust. "Well, the first thing in the morning *I am going on a diet* and sticking to it!"

"In the morning, huh? Well, I will too." Her eyes found the last slice of cake. "But since we already blew it for today, do you want to split that last piece?" she asked hopefully.

Erin looked at the offending beast. "Well. . . ."

"Oh, come on. I don't want to have to throw it out. Trev doesn't like sweets."

"He doesn't?" It was a shame to waste good food when there were so many starving people in the world. "Okay," she said, relenting and reaching for the last piece and dividing it between her and Cathy evenly, "but tomorrow I'm definitely going on a diet!"

It was nearly noon by the time Erin could convince the twins that they should return home and rest for the party that evening. Before she put them down for a brief afternoon nap, she hustled them into her VW and drove to the closest grocery store for a few supplies.

"Now stay close to me and don't get into anything," she warned sternly as they entered the store.

111

"We won't!" they agreed happily. "Can we have some gum, Aunt Erin?"

"I suppose, Huntley," Erin said absently as she studied her shopping list. "Go ahead and pick some out and show it to the lady at the cash register and tell her I'll pay for it along with my other groceries." Maybe that would keep them content until she finished her shopping, she thought hopefully.

They bolted away toward the candy rack and within a few minutes were arguing heatedly over what brand they wanted. Erin kept an ear tuned to the petty squabbling as she selected some fresh produce, sighing hopelessly as the squabble turned into a full-scale assault.

"Stop it this instant!" she warned as she dragged them apart. "Here, you're going to choose this flavor!" A package of banana-flavored bubble gum landed in Huntley's hand. "Now dry up, both of you!"

"What kind is it?" Huntley whined. "Is it them things?" He pointed at the clump of bananas on the wrapping.

"Yes, it's banana. Why?"

Holly set up a wail. "I hate bawnanas!"

"All right, all right! Here. What about cherry?"

Huntley and Holly turned up their noses at the package suspiciously.

"You don't like cherry? Here, try grape. Lemon? Tutti-frutti? Oh, come on! Strawberry . . . how about strawberry?" You would think they were trying to select a rare vintage wine! "It's only gum! Now pick one!"

"Maybe I'll try the bawnana," Holly said.

Erin let out an exasperated breath and handed her the package of gum. Huntley promptly ripped it out of his sister's hand and tore into the wrapper recklessly. In a few minutes they were both chomping away contentedly on wads of bubble gum.

"Stay close," Erin ordered as she went back to her shopping cart.

The meat counter held a tempting selection. Erin stopped and glanced over the fresh ground beef. The twins were getting very tired and fussy now, and she needed to get them home. They had walked beside her peacefully for the last ten minutes, but they were beginning to show signs of discontent. If they could only last a few more minutes, she would be finished. She glanced back over her shoulder and froze. They were standing at the egg case heatedly discussing their preference. Huntley liked scrambled, Holly liked fwied. At the moment neither one liked the other!

"Fwied!"

"Scrambled!"

"Fwied, Huntwey, fwied!" Holly's bubble gum dropped out of her mouth and landed at her brother's feet.

"Scrambled!" he said with deadly determination. He reached down and picked up the bubble gum and stuck it in her brown locks.

"Huntwey Daniels!" she screamed. Her fat hand went for a carton of eggs, a mean scowl on her baby face.

"Holly—no!" Erin threw down the tomato she was holding and bolted toward the egg case in a dead run.

Flying egg missiles flew through the air as a burst of hostilities erupted. Erin ran toward them, her tennis shoes sliding perilously in the sticky, slimy mess. Huntley and Holly were lobbing eggs at each other with Holly screaming at the top of her lungs, mortified at the guck running down her face.

"Don't you throw one more egg!" Erin's feet flew out from beneath her, sending her spiraling into a gigantic display of canned goods. The deafening roar of the display coming down around her shattered the air. The store manager looked up in alarm and dashed toward the melee, waving his arms wildly at the twins.

"Children! Children! My goodness. . . ." His voice died mid-sentence as an egg went sailing past him.

Erin was trying to pick her way out of a hundred cans of fruit cocktail, nearly dying from embarrassment at what was taking place. A few shoppers had pushed their carts into the battle zone but refused to enter the fracas. They stood gaping with their mouths open, occasionally dodging an errant egg.

Erin pulled herself to her feet. "I'm warning you," she swore grimly as she made her way toward the egg-drenched twins, her eyes blazing with savage intensity.

The store manager waded in and took both twins by the scuff of their necks, breaking them apart.

"I'm telling Mommy!" Holly threatened with a loud shriek toward Huntley. She had large tears running down her face, bubble gum stuck in her hair, and egg yolks dripping off every part of her body.

"I'm telling Daddy," Huntley bellowed back, precariously close to tears himself.

"I'm telling Price!" Erin threatened tearfully.

"Aunt Ewin," Holly sobbed, wrapping her arms around Erin's dripping neck, "Huntwey's being naughty again!"

"It wasn't me, Aunt Erin," he cried pitifully, grabbing her around the neck and hanging on wildly. "It was her!"

"Are you all right, lady?" the store manager asked.

"I think so," she mumbled, trying to hold the twins and remain on her feet at the same time. "I'm so sorry about all this . . ." Her voice trailed off as she surveyed the disaster area. How embarrassing!

"Don't worry about it," he said and smiled weakly. "We'll get it cleaned up." Erin knew he wanted to strangle all three of them, but he had pasted his manager's smile on his face and gritted his teeth admirably.

"May I pay for any of the damages?" she asked, shouting above the twins' bawling.

"No, there's no permanent damage," he assured her, ushering her toward the front of the store. Erin was sure he would be relieved to see the last of them.

She loaded them into the VW and left the parking lot with them both crying at the top of their lungs. For the first time in her life, she was deliriously happy that she was deprived of motherhood at the moment!

By the time she had them bathed, had washed the gum out of Holly's hair, and put them down for their afternoon nap, she was near exhaustion. Deciding that a glass of iced tea would make her feel human again, she walked to the refrigerator and opened it. Her mouth dropped open in astonishment. Staring at her was the biggest fish she had ever seen in her life. Its fat, bulgy sides looked monstrous to her as she surveyed it through the clear plastic wrap Price had put around it. My gosh! she mused silently. He really took me seriously when I said to get a large one. There was no way they could eat all that fish.

With a tired sigh she leaned against the open refrigerator door, resentment seeping into her thoughts now as she realized that the fish had not been cleaned yet. She knew he had been in a hurry this morning, but after all, it wasn't her idea to have a fish dinner, and she didn't cherish the idea of cleaning that nasty thing! The mere thought of it made her stomach churn. Cleaning a fish that big would be like slaughtering a hog!

Well, she thought tiredly as she closed the door, she was capable of giving him a meal he would never forget. She sat down at the kitchen table and sipped her iced tea thoughtfully. It seemed very lonely today without Price. She frowned as she thought about what he might be doing right now. She closed her eyes and his face appeared before her. His beautiful green eyes looked back at her, and a contagious smile lit up his handsome features. Price Seaver was a man she could fall in love with, she realized. It startled her that she was ready to admit that. But it was true. He wasn't perfect, but he was close to it. At least as close to it as she was! Okay, time to stop dreaming and start doin'!

Cleaning that fish was the hardest thing Erin had ever attempted. She wrestled it all over the kitchen, alternately holding her nose and gagging. There were very few people in this world whom she would go to this trouble for. In fact, she could only think of one right now, and her thoughts of him were not exactly friendly at the moment. She would give him fair warning, she thought rebelliously as she hacked away relentlessly at the repulsive fish. If he wanted fish again, from now on she would take him to the nearest fast-food seafood restaurant. She wouldn't go through this disgusting mess again for love or money!

After what seemed like hours she had hacked enough pieces off the monster to make a decent mess of fish and threw the remainder in the trash. Her hands were covered with small cuts and her disposition was not at its best. This day had been a nightmare so far, and she still had to get the twins dressed and over to Cathy's by five.

Around three she put a strawberry cake in the oven. A large tossed salad sat in the refrigerator, waiting for the dressing to be added as the final touch. Au gratin potatoes filled a small casserole dish, waiting to go into the oven along with the homemade bread that was rising near the window. Fresh corn on the cob and iced tea should make a meal fit for a king—or a very desirable man, she surmised proudly as she left the kitchen to get herself and the twins ready for the coming evening. Yes, Price Seaver was definitely going to be surprised!

A little before seven Price's car pulled into the drive. Erin's stomach fluttered nervously as he got out. She glanced one last time in the mirror. She had dressed in a white eyelet sundress, a perfect choice to complement her dark tan. Nervously adjusting the small pearl earrings she was wearing, she walked to the door to meet him, feeling almost shy.

"Hi, beautiful," Price said softly as he stepped up on the

porch, his eyes resting boldly on the low cut of her neck-line.

"Hi," Erin responded lightly, her knees feeling very shaky all of a sudden.

"You been keepin' out of trouble, lovely lady?" he asked with a trace of affection in his voice.

"Sure . . . how about you?" She could hardly keep the words from bubbling out of her mouth. Words like, did you see Jeannie? Are you and she going to try again? All those crazy words that were really none of her business, yet the answer meant the world to her. But she said nothing.

"Now what do you think?" He grinned mischievously, watching her eyes turn stormy.

"Sorry I asked," she muttered and turned away to walk to the kitchen.

"You have a headache today?" Price asked as he trailed behind her hurriedly.

"Yes, but I believe it's spelled *t-w-i-n-s,*" she tossed over her shoulder, thinking about the disastrous trip to the grocery store that afternoon.

"Bad day?" he asked sympathetically.

"Don't ask," she warned grimly.

"Where are the little munchkins?" Price glanced around the kitchen.

"Next door at a birthday party."

"You mean we're here alone!" He gave her a suggestive grin. "All by ourselves—alone?"

Dragging out a large cast-iron skillet, Erin ignored his words.

"I hope you're hungry. I fixed your fish dinner." She covered the bottom of the skillet with oil and let it heat while she dipped the pieces of fish into buttermilk, then flour.

"Fish? Well, great!" he said, a little surprised. "I'm

starved. I haven't had any lunch. By the time I took care of my business, I just had time to grab a candy bar."

Erin dropped the fish into the hot oil and watched the pieces as they began to sizzle and turn a mouth-watering brown.

"Hey," Price said, reaching over to take her hand. "Is something wrong? You're very quiet tonight."

Their eyes met, and Erin swallowed hard. He was so virile, so appealing to her at this moment. After the day she had just experienced, she longed to go into his arms and let him hold her, to let him whisper comforting words in her ear.

"No, nothing's wrong. I'm just tired," she murmured, turning back to the fish.

"Anything I can do to help relax you?" He grinned.

"You can sit down and eat like a horse," she said, scooping up some of the fish and laying it on a platter.

"Well, I wasn't exactly thinking along those lines, but if you insist. . . ." He reached over and took a piece of the golden-brown fish and sampled it hungrily. "Boy, this is great!"

Erin smiled smugly to herself as she put more fish in the skillet. Eat your heart out, Jeannie, wherever you are!

"I'll bet you're a little tired yourself, aren't you?" she asked.

"A little," he admitted, sneaking another piece of the fish. "Damn, this stuff's good."

"Thank you. Don't spoil your supper," she cautioned.

"Are you kidding? It would take more than one piece of fish to spoil my appetite!" He reached for another handful. Erin frowned. At this rate there wouldn't be any left to take to Cathy and Trevor.

"I'm sorry I missed you this morning," she said, motioning for him to sit down at the table. "I was next door."

"Yeah, I know. I saw the twins for a minute. Darn! Potatoes, salad, corn on the cob, bread . . . Is that homemade bread?" he asked incredulously as she sliced off thick chunks and buttered them lavishly.

"Sure. You like homemade bread, don't you?"

"I guess. I don't remember eating it very often. You're going to make some man a hell of a wife, Erin." His eyes hungrily surveyed the bountiful table.

I know, Erin thought again smugly.

Price ate hungrily for a few minutes, praising every bite. The fish was disappearing rapidly. "This is the best fish I've ever eaten in my life, Erin. No kidding!" He reached for the platter once more.

"You're going to make yourself sick." She grinned, feeling very good at the moment.

"Which reminds me," he said as he stuffed another bite in his mouth. "After supper I'm going to look in the phone book for the nearest taxidermist to mount *my* fish!" he exclaimed proudly.

Erin was spooning in her au gratin potatoes hungrily. "Your fish?" She smiled.

"I'm telling you, sweetheart, I have *never* enjoyed anything more in my life than the feel of that fish on my line. I worked for twenty minutes to get him in the boat. If John hadn't gotten the net under him when he did, I would have lost him at the last minute." He took another piece of fish. "No kidding, Erin; I wish you could have been there. It's something a man dreams of. It was a Rembrandt on a line!" He sighed proudly. "I spent one whole hour cleaning off a wall in my office where I can hang him."

Erin grinned at him excitedly. "You caught your trophy bass! When?"

Price was still stuffing fish in his mouth at an alarming rate. "When? Why, this morning. Didn't you see it?"

"See it?" Erin frowned. "No, where did you put it?"

"Where? What do you mean?" He glanced up at her in surprise.

"Where did you put your fish?" she repeated, a happy

smile still on her face. "Did John keep it for you until you got back?"

Price looked at her uneasily. "No . . . I left it here."

"Really?" She looked puzzled. "Where?"

"Well, damn, Erin. I don't see how you could have missed it. I put it right there in the refrig—" His face suddenly turned ashen as he dropped his fork and looked down at the half-eaten piece of fish on his plate.

Nausea bubbled up in Erin's throat, her eyes focusing on the empty fish platter.

"Erin," Price's voice sounded very small and childish in the deathly quiet kitchen. "What kind of fish are we eating?"

Erin laid her fork down slowly, her eyes never leaving the fish platter. "I don't know," she answered in a timid voice. "Why?"

"Where did you get it?" he asked hesitantly, his hand starting to tremble as he pushed his chair away from the table and stood up.

She rose to her feet slowly and began backing away from the table, her knees turning to jelly.

"Erin! Answer me," Price roared. "Where did you get this fish we just ate?"

Swallowing hard, she took a deep breath. "From the refrigera—"

"Oh lord, *no!*" Price practically screamed. "*Please* tell me it wasn't the fish I put in the refrigerator before I left this morning!"

Erin was beginning to get very uneasy now. Price didn't look like his normal self at all.

"But I thought you had put that in there for our supper —"

"I *told* Huntley to be *sure* and tell you *not* to touch that fish!"

"He didn't say a thing about not touching that fish, Price! How could you have left a message with a five-year-

120

old concerning anything that important?" she asked incredulously.

"Awww . . . damn, Erin!" Price sank down in his chair. The remains of his beautiful trophy bass lying all nicely browned and greasy on his plate before him suddenly made him feel very, very sick.

"Oh, Price," Erin said, her heart nearly breaking at the agony written on his face.

She kneeled down beside him and laid a consoling hand on his leg. "I'm so sorry. I never dreamed that was your—your trophy bass." If it was possible, she felt as miserable as he did.

Price just sat staring blankly into space. "I *ate* my trophy bass."

"Price, listen," she cried, clutching his arm. "Don't worry about a thing. I'll make arrangements with Cathy to keep the twins overnight, and first thing in the morning you and I will go out and catch you another one!" She tried to keep her voice light and optimistic. He desperately needed that right now. He looked so—so—pitiful!

Price turned dull, expressionless eyes toward her. "Erin. It took me twenty years—twenty *long* years—to catch a fish that size. You think we're just going to go out there in the morning and drag another one in like it just like that?" He snapped his fingers weakly.

"I didn't say it was going to be *easy*," Erin said defensively.

"I thought you told me you were a calm, level-headed person! How could you have cut up my beautiful fish into tiny little pieces . . . and dipped them in flour . . . and throw them in grease. . . ." His voice kept trailing off until there was only a pathetic squeak. "Damn! I think I'm going to be sick!" He stood up, his napkin fluttering unheeded to the floor. "Excuse me, Erin, I think I'm going to lie down for a while. I'm really not feeling very well."

Erin watched helplessly as he walked in a daze over to

the sofa and lay down. As if suddenly remembering his manners, he glanced back up at her and murmured in a polite voice, "Thank you for dinner. It was . . ." Price searched unsuccessfully for the appropriate words, finding none.

"Oh, Price, I feel so awful!" she wailed. "You just get some rest and tomorrow things won't look so bad. You'll see; we'll catch another fish. Just like—"

"Erin, please. Just let me lie here and suffer in peace. Go to bed."

"Are you going to sleep out here tonight?"

"Right now all I want to do is crawl in a hole and scream."

"Would you feel better if I stayed out here with you?"

"No."

She took a deep, sniffling breath. "Are you mad at me?"

"No."

"Can't I do *anything* to help you?"

"No." His voice never changed levels. He was like a zombie.

"Well," she said with a defeated sigh, "I guess I'll go on to bed now."

As she reached the doorway, she turned and glanced back at his morose form lying on the sofa, staring blindly up at the ceiling. "Don't worry . . . darling. We'll catch your fish in the morning." She took another step forward, then paused and looked back again. "Won't we?"

She could barely hear his voice now, but she had no doubt as to what he had said. Only one brief, hopeless word. "No."

CHAPTER SEVEN

The aroma of fresh-perked coffee filled the air as Erin busily packed a small picnic hamper. Glancing toward the clock on the wall, she groaned. Five thirty! Rubbing her eyes tiredly, she slumped back down in her chair, silently willing her sleepy eyes to stay open. In the short time she had been here, she had done more for this infuriating man than she had ever done for anyone in her entire life! What was really irritating was the fact that until the last few days, she hadn't even known him. Now here she sat at five thirty in the morning, trying valiantly to keep her eyes open while she assembled a picnic lunch so she could spend the rest of the day out on a lake she didn't want to be on, fishing uselessly for a fish that had taken twenty years to catch—all because she had wanted to do something nice for a man who in all probability would be married to another woman in a short while.

Erin shook her head wonderingly. "I must have totally lost my mind through all of this!" Heaving a deep sigh, she pushed herself away from the table and reached for a cup. Life had been so much simpler a week ago.

Tiptoeing to the front door, she gazed out at the lake. It still had the same soft, moonlit look it had had when she went to bed. "I have got to try to catch that fish," she said out loud, fretting. She didn't want that bare place on his wall in Memphis on her conscience for the rest of her life! Whether he liked it or not, she was going to at least attempt to catch that stupid fish for him—with or without his help.

Price stirred restlessly on the sofa, bringing Erin back abruptly to the present. She could see the top of his dark, wavy hair barely peeping out over the blanket as he irritably pulled it over his eyes, shading them from the glaring light from the kitchen.

"Erin!" She jumped guiltily as the sound of Price's annoyed voice boomed out. "What!"

"Would you please get that damn light out of my face!" he ordered crisply, his voice muffled by the blanket over his mouth.

"I'm sorry! I'll be leaving in a few minutes," she replied in a miffed tone. She reached for her picnic hamper.

"Why don't you just take your sweet little fanny back to bed and forget that fish!" The voice from under the blanket tent was less sharp now as he turned over on his back, readjusting the pillow Erin had placed under his head the night before.

"What makes you think my mind's on the fish?" she asked resentfully, reaching for her jacket.

"I'm an exceptionally smart man," he said sarcastically. "My trained analytical mind doesn't miss a thing. Where else would you be going at five thirty in the morning with a fishing rod in one hand and a can of worms in the other?"

Throwing back the blanket, he sat up, running his hands through the thick mane of dark, sleep-tousled hair. Erin's breath caught momentarily as her eyes rested briefly on the broad expanse of his bronzed, hairy chest. His powerful muscles played across his arms as he absent-mindedly rubbed sleep-clouded emerald eyes. "I'm serious, Erin; go on back to bed," he said tiredly. He must have taken his shirt off after she covered him last night.

"No," she replied firmly. "*You* go back to sleep." Reaching for the light switch, Erin plunged the room into darkness. She fumbled for the door, banging her way across the room, catching the tip of her rod in the curtains just as she reached the front screen door. "Darn!"

She jerked the tip of the rod twice, nearly bending it double before one strong brown hand snaked out, snatching the rod from her. "I can tell this is going to be one fun day," Price muttered scathingly under his breath as he untangled the rod tip from the curtain. "Are you sure I can't change that pigheaded mind of yours?"

The room was so dark she could barely make out the tall form looming over her. She stared defiantly into the dark. "I'm going!" she hissed.

Letting out a string of expletives, Price bounded back across the room, grabbing his shirt and jerking it on as he talked. "*All right!* We're going to go out there and *prove* you can't catch another eight-pound fish any day of the week. After this useless trip"—Erin could see him pointing his finger at her accusingly—"I don't want to hear another word about it. Is that clear?"

"Perfectly, and no one asked you to go," she pointed out curtly.

"You don't know *one* thing about operating Nathan's fishing boat," Price said, tying his shoes with short, agitated jerks. "Now do you?"

"I can learn," she said, shrugging her shoulders unconcernedly.

"Yeah, sure you could! Ten boat docks could be leveled by the time you got the hang of it."

Erin stiffened, opening her mouth to speak.

"Just don't say *anything,* Erin," Price roared, reaching for the keys to the trunk of his car to get his fishing gear. "I'm going with you!"

By the time they reached the small fishing boat, which was bobbing about in the boat stall, Price was in a worse temper than when they started. Staggering up to the boat, out of breath, he dropped three fishing rods, two tackle boxes, the picnic hamper, the drink cooler, and a bag that held Erin's suntan lotion, insect repellent, sunglasses, two life jackets, her can of worms, and three paperback novels she wanted to read if things got slow.

Giving her a murderous glare, he asked sarcastically, "Are you sure you didn't forget anything?"

Looking intently over the brilliant array assembled before her, Erin's gray eyes grew perplexed. "As a matter of fact, I did mean to bring that extra top I wanted to sun in . . . but," she added quickly, seeing the eyes of the man standing before her suddenly turn violent, "I really don't need it. I can get by just fine without it," she assured him graciously. She handed him the small five-gallon gas can he didn't have room to carry. "Let's go."

Working together as a team, they quickly had the small aluminum fishing boat loaded. The sky was beginning to streak with light as the boat puttered quietly out of the cove. Erin took a deep breath of the fresh early-morning air as the smell of campers' breakfasts reached her nostrils. A large hawk swooped low over the water in front of the boat, its feet barely touching the water before gliding smoothly back up into the early-morning sky. Everywhere she looked there was a peaceful, lazy landscape waiting serenely for the approaching new day to dawn.

Price guided the boat up the lake, the small ten-horse-power motor humming along through the quiet waters, and finally pulling into a small cove some fifteen minutes later. He cut the motor and drifted silently down the quiet bank. The only sounds were the birds chattering noisily in the trees.

"Is this where you caught the other one?" Erin whispered.

Price's back was turned to her as he worked with one of the fishing rods. "Almost."

Erin glanced around, trying to locate a likely spot for a big bass. "Where?" she whispered softly.

"Why are you whispering?" Price asked caustically.

Erin straightened her shoulders swiftly. Why *was* she whispering? "I don't know. It just seems so quiet out here." Her voice seemed to boom across the water.

"Just talk in a normal tone," he advised, handing her a rod with a large fishing plug attached to the line.

Erin looked blankly at the rod for a moment, then back up to Price's gaze. "Where's my worm?"

"If you want those nasty worms on there, you're going to have to put them on yourself," he snapped.

"But no fish in his right mind is going to go for something that looks like that," Erin told him skeptically. "What's the name of this plug?"

"Hawg Frog."

Erin eyed him suspiciously. "You really think a fish will bite this?"

"That's what I caught the other one on," he answered curtly.

"Really?"

"Yes, really," Price mimicked, irritation showing in his voice. "Do you know how to throw it?"

"You don't have to be so hateful," she said as she studied the intricate reel attached to the rod. "Of course I know how to throw it." Brother, was she in trouble now! She had never even seen a reel like this one, let alone thrown one.

Rearing back, she cast out on her side of the boat, her gray eyes widening in fascination as she heard the whirring of the reel. The line snarled in a large, matted ball on the spool.

Price didn't move a muscle, his eyes resignedly taking in the tangled mess. "I thought you said you knew how to throw one," he said in a frosty voice.

"I do!" Erin shot back. "It's just—been awhile, that's all," she finished in a defensive voice. "Just give me a few minutes to get the hang of it."

Price gave a short snort of disgust as she began to unwind the miles of tangled line in the bottom of the boat. Turning back to his rod, he cast smoothly out of the boat, his plug landing neatly at the edge of the bank.

For the next fifteen minutes the little boat drifted down the bank of the cove while Erin worked diligently on her snarled line and Price plugged the shores systematically.

Finally she had a neat reel once more in her hand. She stood up and zealously flung the line out her side of the boat again, making an almost perfect cast. She smiled smugly at Price. "Did you see that?"

"Yes," he answered blandly. "Now which one of us is going to untangle your line off mine?"

Erin's mouth dropped open, her eyes focusing on the two lines tangled together in the water. Immediately one of the two plugs floating together took a sudden dip under the water. Price's reel made a high-pitched whine as line started running through it at a rapid speed. Jumping to his feet, he nearly knocked Erin down as he started cursing, trying desperately to gain control of his rod. Erin began reeling in her line, her fascinated eyes never leaving the churning water as he fought the tangled lines, their eyes catching a glimpse of a large fish breaking the water occasionally.

"Don't reel in, Erin," he screamed in near-hysteria, pushing her firmly down to sit in the boat seat. His fishing line was growing taut now as the fish went deeper into the water. Making his way to the front of the boat, he gave the fish more line, his face a mask of worry. "Boy, this baby's a beauty," he breathed.

Erin's rod began to slide across the bottom of the boat, the tangled lines pulling it along. Picking up the rod, she secretly turned the handle a couple of times, hoping to take some of the slack out to help him.

A sudden snap was heard, then the line on Price's rod flapped loosely in the air, both plug and fish gone!

With a disgusted snort he turned quickly and saw Erin's rod in her hand. "Did you reel in your line?"

Crossing both fingers, Erin hedged slightly. "No, my rod just started sliding across the boat, so I picked it up."

He sat back down on the front boat seat, skeptically watching her as he opened his tackle box for another plug. "That was a hell of a fish," he muttered under his breath.

Erin sheepishly rolled her line back in, her plug still intact. "Did your other one really weigh eight pounds?" she asked conversationally.

"Nearly nine," he confirmed gloomily.

"Wow, that *was* a nice one, wasn't it," she complimented him.

"Wasn't it though," he remarked dryly, casting out once again on his side of the boat. "Look, you fish toward the back on your side; I'm going to throw up toward the front," he instructed. "That way there shouldn't be any reason for a repeat of what just happened, should there?" he finished pointedly.

"None whatsoever!" she agreed enthusiastically.

For the next two hours they fished together quietly, saying very little to each other except for the two times her line got hung up, plus the three times she lost her plug.

As Price was tying on her fourth plug of the day, he gave her some friendly advice. "You'd better marry a millionaire if you intend to fish any after you're married!"

Later in the morning Price caught a nice-size bass and Erin held the net for him as he brought it up alongside the boat. "Ooooh," she squealed excitedly, "that's a *big* one."

Price held it up with his hands for closer inspection. "Yeah, that's not bad."

"How much do you think this one weighs? Almost as much as the other one?" she asked hopefully.

He shot her a disgusted look. "This bass won't weigh over two pounds, Erin."

"It certainly looks bigger than that," she told him, hoping to boost his confidence. "Don't you think you could have this one mounted to put on the empty wall in your office?"

Price turned incredulous green eyes on her. "Mount a two-pound fish?"

"Well . . . it might look impressive on your wall," she said, still holding to the slim hope that this fish might satisfy him.

"Yes, I could also nail ten minnows on a board and draw big mouths on them for a conversation piece, but I'd rather hold out for a bigger bass, if you don't mind," he said, throwing the smaller fish back into the water.

"Why did you let him go?" Erin protested. "I could have fried him for sup—oh," she said, sitting back down in her seat. "I guess you've lost your taste for fish, huh?"

"Forever," he agreed bluntly.

Erin reached down, resignedly opening the picnic hamper. "Are you getting hungry?"

"I could probably eat. What have you got in there?" he asked, peering into the wicker basket.

"Tuna salad sandwich," Erin admitted. "Remember, I didn't know you were coming," she added defensively.

"Haven't you got anything else?"

"Crackers, a candy bar, a doughnut and some pretzels."

"Good lord, do you eat like that all the time?" he questioned disgustedly. "You must have a cast-iron stomach."

Erin was munching along contentedly on her sandwich now, unruffled by his criticism. "Do you want half this sandwich or not?" she asked him again patiently. "It's going fast."

"Give me half of the stupid thing," Price said roughly.

Erin broke the sandwich in two pieces and handed him one. "I suppose Jeannie packs a more nutritionally balanced lunch," she said snidely, handing him a can of soda she had extracted from the cooler.

130

"That wouldn't be too hard," he responded, grinning for the first time today. "But come to think of it—yes, she's a real good cook."

"Naturally," Erin said curtly.

"And," Price added, "she dresses nice, she can sew her own clothes, she dances well, she. . . ." He paused and grinned. "Come to think of it," he said, pondering, "I don't know of a thing she doesn't do well." He wadded his napkin and pitched it playfully at her. "Want to split your doughnut?"

"You can have all of it," Erin offered, her appetite fading. "Did you have a nice time in Memphis?"

"Not particularly," Price returned, tearing the doughnut in two and biting into the soft, cream-filled center.

"Did you see Jeannie?" Erin cast her eyes down to her half-eaten sandwich. She had to know.

Price was silent for a moment as he chewed thoughtfully on his dessert, staring out across the water. The silence was uncomfortable until he decided to answer her question. "Yes, she came to the office."

An acute pain tore through Erin. She had known deep down that he would see her. So why did it hurt so badly? "Did you have a long talk?" she asked quietly.

"I suppose we did." He was still staring out at the blue water, his face an unreadable mask. He glanced up at Erin. "We had a long talk . . . and I kissed her."

Erin flinched and turned away from him. Why was he doing this? She didn't want to know that. She laid her sandwich down on the boat seat, her appetite completely gone now.

"Don't you want to know what happened after that?" he asked softly.

"No," she answered honestly, fighting the tears that threatened to form in her eyes.

"Well, I'm going to tell you anyway. I kissed her—and I didn't feel anything. Nothing, Erin."

131

"I'm sorry," Erin said, still keeping her eyes from him. "Maybe the feeling will come back. She wants to try again, doesn't she?"

"Yes, she suggested that."

"What did you say?" Erin's gaze finally found his.

"I told her I'd have to think about it."

"Oh." Her stomach felt queasy.

"What would you say, Erin, if Quinn wanted you back?" he asked calmly.

Erin was surprised by his question. What would she say? At one time she would have given her very life for that opportunity. But now?

"I don't want him to ask me back," she admitted tiredly. "I don't love him any longer. Maybe I never really did. Maybe it was a silly high school crush that took six years to get over."

Price reached out and touched her face with his hand, his eyes caressing her tenderly. "I'm glad to hear that, lovely lady. When I said that I kissed Jeannie and didn't feel anything, I meant that, Erin. It surprised the hell out of me, but I didn't feel a thing for her."

Tears were threatening to overflow as she brought her hand up to touch his. "I'm glad." She smiled.

"You are? As old friends, I thought you might want me to get back with Jeannie and you could meet her sometime," he said, stroking the line of her jaw lightly.

"As an old *friend*, I might. We could even ask Quinn to join us," she replied. "I'm sure you'd really like him once you got to know him, Price."

"I doubt that!" Price said irritably, his hand dropping from her cheek rapidly. "Well, back to the old grind, Holmes. I want to get this silly fishin' trip over with."

The afternoon dragged by in a blaze of heat. Erin had on a layer of suntan lotion an inch thick, yet her nose was still bright red. The hot sun beat down on them unmercifully. She took an empty soda can, filled it with water from

132

the lake and poured the cooling liquid over her steaming body, giving her some relief from the scorching sun. Price glanced up, his eyes going to the front of her wet blouse. The water had turned the fabric into a transparent delight, bringing a wicked grin to his already flushed face.

"What are we doing? Having dessert again?" he asked dryly as he languorously let his gaze roam seductively over the outline of her generous breasts.

Erin had been deep in thought as she looked up and met his intense scrutiny. "What?"

"I said, what are you doing?"

"Sitting here sweating. What are you doing?" she returned shortly, wondering if the sun had finally cooked his brain.

"I'll tell you what I'm *going* to be doing if you don't stop pouring water over the front of your blouse," he answered with a devious grin.

Erin gasped and swiftly raised her arms protectively across the front of her blouse. "I'm sorry! I didn't realize. . . ."

"Don't let it worry you. I probably wouldn't have mentioned it, except I knew you would be wondering why I was panting and drooling in another five minutes," he dismissed grumpily. "For a troll, you've got one of the best sets of—"

"Price!"

"What?"

"Just stick to your fishing," she warned grimly.

"Is your line tangled again?" Price asked, changing the subject abruptly.

"I think so," she said meekly, heaving a sigh. "I'll just sit here until you're ready to go."

Price cast a few more times, ignoring her. He wouldn't care if I sat here and rotted, she thought miserably.

Finally he laid his rod down carefully and asked, "You ready to throw in the towel yet?"

"Yes," Erin acknowledged gratefully. She would go to her grave with the black stigma of having fried his irreplaceable fish! She might as well face it.

"Hand me your rod, then," he said tiredly, his face flushed from the heat.

Gladly relinquishing the hated stick, she handed it to him gingerly, not wanting to tangle it more than it already was. He gave a few quick, agitated jerks, but the line remained securely buried, hooked to a dead limb sticking out of the water. Growing increasingly impatient, he worked fruitlessly for the next five minutes, muttering selected uncomplimentary phrases under his breath, giving one final authoritative and no-nonsense jerk. The plug came careening back toward the occupants of the small boat with lightning speed. Erin ducked rapidly as she heard the whistle of the plug sailing past her head. It ricocheted off the stern light at the very moment that Price swung his head around to watch the path of the flying missile, which came sailing back, catching him squarely on the arm. Erin's gasp of disbelief echoed through the quiet cove as Price stood stunned in the front end of the boat, the plug embedded above his elbow.

Springing into action, she lunged for him. "Oh, Price, darling, hold still," she cried sympathetically. "I'll try to get it out!"

Price's shocked expression changed to one of pure terror now as he backed frantically away from her outstretched hands. "*No!*" he gasped. "Don't you dare touch it!"

"But Price," she said with a shudder, "it's stuck in your arm. We *have* to do something!" Although Erin was a nurse and supposed to remain calm in situations such as this, it was an entirely different story when someone you loved was involved!

Snapping out of his stunned state, Price reached out, putting his uninjured arm around her, the fishing plug hanging grotesquely off his other arm. "Calm down, sweetheart. I'm all right. You can't just try to get it out. It has several barbs in it."

Patting him tenderly, she said consolingly, "Just relax and we'll go back to the house. Then I'll run you over to the hospital. They'll take it out in five minutes." She sucked in her breath and gave him a sympathetic pained look, concern clouding her troubled eyes as he seated himself back at the motor. "Oh, darling, does it hurt very much?"

Price chuckled ironically. "Only when I move it. But I don't plan on moving it around too much in the next couple of hours," he assured her solemnly.

He started the small engine and drove using his good hand, heading for the boat dock as fast as the undersize fishing rig would take them. They had barely reached the dock before Erin was out of the boat and racing up the hill for the keys to her car, with Price following slowly behind. Bolting back through the front door of the house, she practically shoved him into the passenger side of the Volkswagen, despite his loud protests. "I'm not hurt, I tell you. Just calm down!"

The red bug sprang into life as Erin ground it into gear, peeling out of the drive, floorboarding the gas pedal and flying out onto the blacktop road. Price grabbed frantically for the handle on the car's dash for support. The little car's motor still had a miss in it, causing Erin to really have to give it gas to get up any speed. Driving faster than she had ever dreamed she could, Erin screeched the Volkswagen around curves, up and down hills, making her small car a red blur on the winding roads.

Price was clutching the dash, his face growing paler by the minute.

For the next forty-five minutes she fought her way through the heavy resort traffic, her pace sometimes slowing to a crawl, and at one point sitting for a full ten minutes without moving, drumming her nails on the steering wheel. Heaving an exasperated sigh, she spied a small space on the right-hand side and swung the Volkswagen around the piled-up traffic, leaning on her horn as she careened madly around the sitting cars. Price groaned audibly, laying his head back on the headrest, clamping his eyes tightly shut.

"Don't worry, darling," she mumbled reassuringly. "We're almost there!"

Irate drivers blared their horns and shook their fists as Erin gunned her way past them, loose gravel flying up on all their windshields.

Wheeling breathlessly up to the emergency entrance, Erin skidded to a sliding halt. Price opened his eyes cautiously, letting out a relieved sigh. "Do you always drive like that?" he asked in a shaky voice.

Looking earnestly into his pained gaze, she answered piteously, "I'm sorry it took so long—my car's not running right!"

Price's face was a mask of disbelief as she helped him from the car. "Erin," he snapped briskly, "there's nothing wrong with my legs. I can walk!" She nevertheless put a protective arm around him and urged him to lean on her as they pushed open the doors to the emergency room.

The nurse on duty glanced up, quickly assessed the situation and handed Erin a clipboard for her to fill out for hospital records, instructing firmly, "You fill these out, and"—pointing to Price—"you follow me." They disappeared behind a closed door, leaving Erin standing alone in the antiseptic-smelling waiting room. She sank down on the straight-backed chair and stared blankly at the papers before her.

Beginning to laugh almost hysterically, her mind mocked this impossible situation. She couldn't fill out any of these papers; she didn't know anything about him! Wasn't that crazy! She giggled. This man who had walked into her life barely four days ago and quietly stolen her heart hadn't even told her where he lived in Memphis or anything personal about himself at all. Jeannie would know these things, but Erin didn't.

She brushed away a stray tear and filled in his name and the address he was staying at presently, leaving the rest of the sheet blank. She watched a white-coated doctor walk swiftly through the door Price had entered a few minutes before. Thirty minutes later the uniformed nurse walked back out the door, a smile lighting her motherly face.

"Everything's just fine, Mrs. Seaver. Your husband will be ready to leave shortly. The doctor's just finishing up."

Erin smiled weakly, her emotions totally drained. "Is he all right?"

"Why, he's just fine, honey," the nurse assured her. "These things happen all the time down here." Noting the strained look on Erin's face, she asked concernedly, "Mrs. Seaver, are *you* all right?"

"I'm all right," Erin said tiredly, not bothering to correct her mistake. "I'm afraid my—uh—husband will have to fill the remainder of these papers out." Her gray eyes briefly met the puzzled ones of the nurse. "We haven't been married very long," Erin explained meekly.

"Well, no problem," the nurse said. "Here he comes now."

Jumping to her feet, Erin hurried to Price. His arm came out to enfold her in a comforting hug. "It's all right, honey," he said softly. "You can get that terrified look off your face now."

"Are you sure you're all right?" she asked, hugging him in a tight, possessive embrace.

"Well," he told her in a low tone, "I may need some private nursing after a while, but let's get out of here first."

"Not so fast, Mr. Seaver," the nurse piped up. "Your wife wasn't able to complete the hospital forms." She

137

motioned for him to step over to her desk, where Price filled in the needed information.

As they walked back out into the cooler air of the fall night, he looked down at her and grinned. "Wife, huh?"

Erin blushed. "I didn't want to embarrass her."

He gave her a reassuring squeeze. "I kind of liked it. Where's the car keys?"

She looked up swiftly, surprise clouding her features. "Why?"

"Because I'm driving home!"

"Well, for heaven's sake, why? And what about your arm?" She thought she had done a tremendous job of driving to get him here.

Price glanced at her sternly. "My arm is fine, and you drive like a demented jockey!"

Erin stiffened, resentment overcoming her. That was gratitude for you! She had practically risked her life to get him here in record time, and he was standing there criticizing her driving!

Hooking one arm around her neck, he pulled her head over to his. Grinning cockily, he lightly kissed her pouting mouth. "Now don't get your feathers ruffled. I'd just rather drive home and let you rest. You've had a hell of a day," he added tenderly.

Too tired to argue, Erin laid her head down on his broad shoulder, only too glad to turn things back over to his strong, capable hands. She slept during the drive home, snuggled close against him.

Her last coherent thought was that she had made such a terrible mess out of things. True, she had set out to impress Price. And undoubtedly she had impressed him, although not in the way she had hoped to. But at least he had come back from Memphis . . . at least she had that much.

CHAPTER EIGHT

The peaceful sounds of night floated quietly through the open window as Erin tossed restlessly back and forth. Since coming to bed an hour ago, she had been unable to turn her thoughts off and go to sleep. Her nerves were tense from the harrowing day she had just been through. By the time she had gotten the twins in bed, she had been almost numb with fatigue. Price had helped her tuck them in, then retired to his bedroom, the strain of the traumatic day showing on his sunburned face.

Erin sat up and tossed the light blanket back, then listened to the croaking tree frogs for a moment. Why couldn't she sleep? Why did her mind refuse to shut down and grant her some peace? After all the solemn promises she had made to herself about not becoming involved with another man—especially one who reminded her so vividly of the past—she found herself right back in the same old prison—a prison in which she loved the man and he didn't return that love.

Heaving a long sigh, she ran her fingers through her hair. At least Price had been honest. She had known from the start that he was in love with another woman. Her only mistake had been allowing her defenses to break down and open her heart to another man. It was a humdinger of a mistake, no doubt, but nonetheless she had made it!

Realizing that sleep was impossible, she slipped out of

bed and into her housecoat. She couldn't keep lying here, her mind running over all her mistakes. The house was quiet as she tiptoed through the kitchen and let herself out the back door silently. The moon lit the night brightly as she walked down the path leading to the bluff that over-looked the lake.

A gentle breeze ruffled her hair as she stopped and stared out over the water. The lake lay shimmering in the muted darkness like a rare and beautiful jewel. The lights of hundreds of other homes in the area twinkled back at her brightly. Leaning against a tree, she tried to envision who lived in those houses and if they were happy. Her hand brushed against the steps of a wooden ladder as her eyes caught the shadowy form of the twins' tree house in its branches . . . the one Price had helped to build. Tucking the hem of her gown up around her waist, she began to climb up the stairs slowly, feeling her way ahead of herself in the dark with one hand. When she reached the level platform, her heart nearly stopped as her fingers came in contact with a bare foot! A loud gasp filled the night air as a dark form shot up, grabbing her groping hand. Erin let out a terrified scream and shoved frantically at the scary bulk, sending it spiraling over the side of the hay-covered platform. A man's voice, mouthing some very unfriendly phrases, could be heard as he hit the ground with a jarring thud.

Erin's heart was pounding as she crawled to the side and peeked over, trying to make out the identity of the intruder.

"Price! Is that you?" she hissed.

"Damn it, Erin! What are you doing out here at this hour of night?" Price sat up and rubbed the small of his back, obviously in pain.

"What am *I* doing out here? What are *you* doing out here? I thought you were asleep hours ago," she whispered loudly.

140

"I couldn't sleep," he said as he pushed himself to his feet slowly, "so I came out here to think."

About Jeannie, I'll bet! Erin fumed as she scooted over to make room for him as he climbed back up the ladder.

Price reached the hay-covered platform and stretched out with a groan. "Damn . . . I think you've broken my back!"

"You should have let me know you were up here!" she snapped. "You nearly scared me to death!"

"I didn't even hear you walk up! I must have finally dozed off," he muttered defensively, still rubbing his aching back.

"Oh, here! Turn over," she grumbled, shoving him on his side. "I'll rub it for you."

Price rolled over on his stomach gratefully. She pulled his shirt up and began to massage his lower back. Erin's hands worked slowly, and the feel of his bare skin against her fingertips sent tiny shivers racing up her spine. He felt so warm and vibrantly alive. She wondered what it would feel like to touch him everywhere.

"What are you doing out here?" he asked contentedly. "I thought you were asleep."

"No, I couldn't sleep," she admitted, stroking him gently.

"Any particular reason?"

"No, I suppose I was too tired."

"Your hands feel good," he said softly. "If I married you, would you promise in the wedding vows to do this to me at least twice a day?" he asked lightly.

Among other things. She grinned silently to herself but ignored his question. "It's really pretty out here at night," she said as she gazed out over the water. "Is that a boat sitting out there in that cove?"

Price turned his head so he could see the lake. "Yeah, that's a sailboat . . . it's anchored out there. Can you hear that bell?"

141

Erin listened above the sounds of the night and could hear the faint tinkle of a bell as the boat bobbed up and down in the water. "Yes, I hear it."

"It's tied to the top of the mast. I had a heck of a time figuring out where the sound was coming from," Price whispered.

"It sounds nice." She sighed. "Everything sounds so peaceful and quiet out here. I'll miss it when I go back to the city."

"When are you going back?" he asked quietly.

"Sunday. Brenda and Nathan should be home sometime late in the afternoon."

Her hands slipped sensuously across his broad shoulders. She could feel the strong columns of muscle as she kneaded the bare, warm flesh. It struck her that she would like to kiss along the same path that her fingers had just covered. She wanted to taste the saltiness of his skin to see if he tasted as good as he smelled.

"What's waiting for you at home, Erin Holmes?" he inquired in a drowsy voice.

"My job at the hospital, a little apartment, some very nice friends . . ."

"Men?"

"All kinds," she said evasively. "I have both men and women friends."

"What's your job at the hospital?" He rolled over on his back and took her hands in his, his eyes meeting hers in the moonlight. "Tell me about yourself, lovely lady. What makes you tick?"

"Oh, you don't want to hear the boring story of my life." She laughed. Her hands trembled slightly in his.

"Yes, I do," he insisted. "I want to know all about you."

"Really?" she asked, staring into the magical depths of his sleepy eyes.

"Yeah, really." He pulled her head down on his chest and lay back. "Now . . . are you a janitor at the hospital, do you clean bedpans, or do you do brain surgery?" he coaxed as he gently stroked her hair.

"I'm a nurse in a pediatrics ward. A very good one, I might add."

"I figured as much. You're much too good with children never to have been around them before. Do you like your job?"

"Very much. I love children. There are times when I think I'll die with grief over some of their terrible illnesses, but at other times I thank God that I can be there to hold them in my arms and love them when they're alone and frightened in the middle of the night."

"And who holds *you* in their arms and tells you they love you when you're alone and frightened at night?" he asked gently.

"No one," she admitted. "But someday somebody will."

"Someday when the perfect man comes along."

"He will," she said firmly. "I used to lie in bed at night when Brenda and I were in high school and build the perfect man in my mind. He would be tall, dark and handsome. We would live in a little house outside the city and I would take care of his children. We would grow old together. After our children were grown, we'd still love each other as much as the first day we married. No—more! Much more. When we were ninety, he would still be my only love. We would live a simple, full life, and when it was time for us to leave this old earth, we would simply lie down somewhere together and never wake up."

"And you thought you had found that in Quinn?" he asked tenderly.

"Yes. Oh, *now* I know that I didn't, but then . . . well, you see, I never did attract the boys like Brenda did," she admitted readily. "Brenda was always the one with the looks, and boys used to flock to her."

Price shook his head thoughtfully. "Brenda's okay, but

I don't see where you think she's anything exceptional. In my opinion, you're the good-looking one!"

Erin raised up and looked at him in amazement. "Are you teasing me again?"

"Hell, no, I'm not teasing you! Why do you always come down so hard on yourself?"

"I don't know," she said with a deep sigh, laying her head back down on his broad chest. "I've always been very insecure about my looks."

"Well, don't be. You're the prettiest woman I've ever held like this," he assured her as his hands drew her tighter to him.

"I suppose you've held a lot . . . I mean, other than Jeannie." She closed her eyes and savored the feel of being in his arms.

"Can't say that I have. I'm usually a one-woman man. To be honest, I can't handle more than one at a time." He chuckled intimately.

Erin's hold on him tightened. "Please, Price, I don't want to talk about you being—intimate with anyone." Her voice trailed off weakly.

"Why?"

"I don't know why . . . I just don't."

"Well, I hadn't planned on giving you a detailed account of my previous love life, but it intrigues me to know why it would upset you."

"I told you, I don't know either!" She shifted around irritably. "Let's drop the subject."

"Nope. I want to talk about it. Why should you care how many women I've gone to bed with?" he persisted.

"Price!" Erin sat up and glared angrily at him. "This is crazy!"

"So? Mark it off to being alone in the moonlight with a beautiful woman." Erin was shocked when he grinned and reached for her. "Come here and kiss me, troll."

"You're scaring me," she warned, but she went willingly into his outstretched arms.

They kissed for a moment, a warm, exploring kiss.

"You're scaring me now," he whispered huskily as their mouths began to search hungrily for each other.

"Why?"

"Erin, I just came out of one damn mess. I don't know if I'm ready to jump right back into another one." His breathing took on a quickened pace as she pressed her body tightly against his.

"Are you going back to Jeannie?"

"Oh, brother! Do we have to talk about Jeannie right now?" His eyes found hers in the moonlight. "Don't look at me that way."

"What way? I'm only *looking* at you." Erin kissed his eyes closed. "There, does that help?"

"No. I think you need to kiss here." He pointed to his cheek. "And here, and here. . . ."

"And here, and here. . . ." Erin took over, her hands wrapping securely around his neck. She was tired of fighting her feelings. She was hopelessly in love with this man, and after tonight he would probably suspect it. He might not be able to make a commitment, but her heart had already made hers.

"Uh, I think you'd better be careful. . . ." Price whispered against her lips. "It's been awhile since I've—"

"I told you I don't want to talk about that!"

"But I'm afraid you're going to take advantage of me." He grinned sweetly.

"And you'd care?" Her tongue traced the outline of his lips.

"No, if you promise you'll still respect me in the morning." His teeth nipped playfully at her nose.

"I'll respect you as much as I always have."

Price frowned. "What do you mean by—" His words were cut off by her mouth closing over his.

Five minutes later they lay in each other's arms completely nude, bare skin pressed against bare skin yearningly. It hadn't taken them long to undress each other. As each item of clothing had fallen away from Erin's body, Price had kissed that area tenderly, his hands running gently over her feminine curves.

The feel of his hair-roughened chest mashed tightly against the fullness of her breasts now made Price and Erin realize just how long it had been for both of them. Erin's fingers lovingly touched the bare skin of his back, her lips tasting the hollows of his neck, breathing in the clean, male scent of him. For one small moment sanity returned to Erin as she thought about what the consequences could be from the spontaneous lovemaking, but she soon relaxed, remembering she would be safe.

"I knew your skin would feel like this," he said with a groan as his hands ran down the length of her satiny thighs. He gave her a long, lazy kiss, stoking the growing fire between them even higher. Cupping her bare bottom with one large hand, he pulled her against the proof of his desire for her. "I want you, Erin. I want you more than I've even let myself believe."

Waves of desire coursed through her as she pressed against the male length of him, his body imprisoning hers in a web of growing arousal. His lips brushed her nipples before his tongue explored the rosy peaks with slow expertise, bringing them to pebble hardness.

Slowly his hands moved downward, skimming the sides of her rib cage, dropping down to tenderly caress her firm stomach.

"Do you honestly not realize how very lovely and desirable you are to a man, Erin? Hasn't a man ever told you how your skin feels like silk, how your hair smells like roses, how your lips taste honey sweet. . . ." He moaned as his mouth took hers again roughly.

Her hand reached out shyly to touch him, and his body

146

tensed, then melted against hers as he groaned once more, his kisses growing more urgent, more uncontrolled.

She didn't protest as he slid her beneath him and she felt him inside her, gently at first, then he began to move slowly. Together they shared a height of passion both had never known before, one they had only dreamed they would someday find. Price was a tender yet masterful lover, blending his body with hers in an act of love. Soaring higher and higher, their bodies met in perfect rhythm, perfect harmony. At this moment he was her perfect man in every way that mattered.

As Erin cried out for release, Price's arms held her tight as tremors shook their bodies, melting away the last of their tension and frustration. When at last they were able to speak, it was in whispered murmurs as they lay wrapped in each other's arms. Contentment and peace flowed between them as she lay in the haven of his embrace.

The bright moon played across her face as she opened her eyes and stared up into the sky filled with a million glittering stars. There was no need for words. What had just taken place between them was a rare and beautiful thing, and she only wanted to savor the hour.

"Price."

"Humm."

"I—was it—I mean—"

"Was it something special?" he supplied drowsily. "Was it something other than the fact I haven't been with a woman in a very long time? Yes, lovely Erin, it was something special."

Erin rolled back over to look at him. "Were you *really* celibate all that time?"

Price chuckled. "Don't look at me like it was hereditary. Yes, I was. I haven't had any particular interest in a woman since Jean—in a long time."

"I know, since Jeannie—oh, my gosh!" Erin gasped and

sat straight up. "Your arm! I completely forgot about your hurt arm. Why didn't you say something, Price? Why didn't you stop me!"

"Now, Erin," Price said calmly, cocking a dark eyebrow at her seriously. "Do I look like a stupid man to you?"

"Well, no, but the way we've been holding each other— well, that had to hurt!" She was flabbergasted that she could have forgotten his injury. "Didn't it?"

"Like hell. But it was worth it."

Her fingers reached out to touch the swelling on his arm. "I can't believe you wouldn't say something," she murmured.

"If you're waiting for me to kick you out of my bed, you'll be waiting a long time," he warned, nipping at her fingers.

"Are you sure you're not hurt?"

"Kiss it here." He pointed to his arm.

Erin touched her lips to the spot he pointed at and breathed a kiss there. "Better?"

"I think I feel better all over." He sighed, pulling her across his muscled chest. "You didn't bring any blankets with you by any chance, did you? This is the first time I can recall lying out on a riverbank in September, nude, with an oversexed troll, a swollen arm and a broken back. Are you getting a little chilly?"

"Here, put my housecoat over you," she offered, scooting around on the hay to find her discarded robe.

"That thing! Oh, come on, Erin!" Price grumbled as she found the garment and laid it over both of them.

"Stop squirming around, Price, or you're going to fall out again," she warned.

"What if someone would happen to see us? I look like a fool with this flimsy thing thrown over me. Besides, I'd have more warmth with just a pair of socks on," he said fretfully as she lay back down and hugged him close.

"You didn't wear your socks, remember?"

"Ahh . . . yes, I remember. Did I wear my pants?"

"Of course you did. Silly!"

"Then why am I lying here wrapped in a woman's negligee half-naked?"

"Because you just made love to a very—needy woman," she teased, brushing her lips against his lightly.

"That's right, I did, didn't I? And she made me a very happy man."

They exchanged several long kisses, happy to be in each other's arms.

"I wonder if Brenda and Nathan are having as much fun as we are right now," Price whispered.

"Sure they are. They have a perfect marriage, no matter what you say," Erin reminded him.

"Oh, yes, I'm sure they've spent the entire week in tranquil bliss," Price said. "You're a dreamer, lovely lady!"

"So? What can it hurt? Someday I'll find my perfect man, Price Seaver, and when I do, you'll be the first to know." She caressed his smooth jaw lovingly. "Yes, you'll be the first to know," she finished softly to herself.

Price lay quietly, his hand stroking the bare flesh of her arm thoughtfully. "I hope you do." He closed his eyes regretfully. Why couldn't he tell her what he was feeling right now? Had Jeannie made him so bitter about life that he couldn't tell this wonderful woman how he really felt? Would he ever be able to commit himself again?

"Maybe I'd better go in and check on the twins," Erin said sleepily. "I know we can hear them, but if they woke up and were frightened of the dark . . ."

"Not for another few minutes," Price pleaded huskily, his arms tightening possessively around her. "It's late and they're sleeping soundly. Stay in my arms for just a little longer, Erin."

She leaned down and kissed him, the fires of passion

building quietly in them once more. His hands reached out to bring her body back to his. Their gazes met, and the world stopped spinning as his eyes sent her a private message, one that only a man can send to a woman. It spoke of love, of wanting, of uncertainty, of pain. The gentleness of his gaze was like a soft caress as she lay with him again on the sweet-smelling hay. It was a gentle coming together this time, a slow, languid time of making love to each other, of discovering each other's likes, dislikes. When the ecstasy had again mounted to unbearable proportions, the world shattered into a million glowing stars once more. They lay in each other's arms, spent and exhausted, their legs intertwined, and listened to the sound of the water lapping gently against the shoreline.

"What should we do tomorrow?" Price asked as Erin threatened to succumb to the numbed sleep of a satisfied lover.

"I don't know. Any suggestions?"

"It's Saturday. Let's take the twins on a picnic, maybe go swimming. I'd like to spend another day with them before I leave for Memphis."

Erin tensed at his words. Tomorrow would be their last day together. "Whatever you want. Maybe we could take them out to eat tomorrow night, then to a movie?"

"I don't think we'd better plan on taking them out, sweetheart. If I remember right, Huntley eats like a bulldozer out of control."

Erin giggled, thinking about the twins' less than perfect table manners. Price rolled over and faced her. "Why don't you and I spend the evening alone. I'll arrange for a baby-sitter and we'll go to some quiet, secluded, out-of-the-way place—just you and me. What do you say, Auntie Ewin?"

"I say that sounds wovewy, Uncle Pwice," she lisped. "We'll spend the day with the children, and the night will be for—each other." Her hand traced the outline of his face affectionately. "Thank you for making me feel like a woman again tonight. I haven't felt that way for a very long time."

"My pleasure. Remind me to give you my business card, and if I can ever be of assistance, give me a call." He gave her a sexy wink.

Erin pushed him playfully as he reached out and poked her in the ribs.

"Price! Don't do that. I'm ticklish!"

"Oh, really?" He grinned at her wickedly. "Where? Here?"

"Price!" she gasped, grabbing for both his hands.

"How about here? Here?"

"Stop, you fool!" Erin reached out and grabbed thin air as she felt herself teetering on the edge of the small platform. "Price! We're going to fa—" Her voice faltered in mid-air as they both tumbled out of the tree house simultaneously. Erin landed on top of Price in a heap, nearly knocking the breath out of both of them.

"Oh, damn! I *know* you broke my back this time—and my arm" he said with a moan as she tried to get up off him but developed a strange case of the giggles.

"Stop laughing and get off me!" he thundered, making her laugh even harder. If anyone found them in this ridiculous situation, she would die of embarrassment!

"*What is so funny!* Get your elbow out of my stomach— Erin!" Tears were running down her face now, she was laughing so hard. "I'm going to make it a cardinal rule never to go to bed with anyone crazier than I am," Price said with a snort, her laughter growing contagious. "Erin! Get your hands off my—you're nuts, lady, right down nuts!"

She reached over and hugged his neck tightly, her body shaking with hilarity. "Oh, Price, I like you so very much!" She didn't want to say "love." It would scare him to death. "You're the best friend I've ever had!"

"Yeah, well, I like you, too, you crazy woman."

"Really?" Her laughter was losing momentum now as she wiped at the tears in her eyes.

"Really." His gaze met hers again tenderly. "I just don't know what in the devil I'm going to do about it."

"Will you let me know when you find out?" she asked solemnly.

"Oh, I'm sure you'll be the first to know, lovely lady. I'm sure you'll be the first to know."

CHAPTER NINE

"Aunt Ewin, Huntwey's eatin' the stick of budder."

Erin turned from the stove and gave him a stern look. "Huntley, put the butter back down on the dish and eat your cereal—please."

"When is Mommy comin' home?" he asked as he laid the stick of margarine back on the dish obediently.

Holly dropped her fork and swiftly brought her hand out in front of her, folding down all her fingers until she only had the small one left. "Tomowwow."

"That's right, tomorrow." Erin tried not to let her voice sound too relieved. "How would the two of you like to go on a picnic today?"

Neither one exhibited much enthusiasm as they spooned their hot cereal into their mouths.

"Is this Saturday?" Huntley asked worriedly.

"Yes, why?" Erin sat down at the table with her cup of coffee.

"Do we gotta go to Sunday school in the morning?" Holly asked with a long sigh.

"Don't you go every Sunday?"

"Yes, but Huntwey's unwuly there—weally bad!"

"I am not!" he denied indignantly.

"You are too! You're not supposed to talk out woud, and you *always* do!"

"Why not? Who's going to stop me?" He cocked his head arrogantly.

"Aunt Ewin will have to make them daddies stop you!"

"What daddies?" he scoffed.

"Them daddies that always come by with them dishes and make people put money in them. Them daddies called hushers, Huntwey!" she scolded in a loud, no-nonsense tone.

"Children, stop your arguing and eat your breakfast. When Uncle Price gets up, he's going to take us on a picnic," Erin interrupted hurriedly.

"Is he *still* sweepin'?" Holly bit into her toast disinterestedly.

"Yes, he was up very late last night." Erin let her thoughts run deliciously back to a few hours earlier. It had been close to dawn when they finally came back into the house. She smiled lovingly as she recalled how passionate, how demanding, yet how very sweet Price had been.

"I wike him," Holly decided, licking the jelly off her sticky fingers. "Don't you wike him too, Aunt Ewin?"

"Very much, Holly. He's a nice man."

The sound of a car coming up the drive and the angry slam of a door caught Erin's attention. As she started toward the window to peer out, the kitchen door flew open and Brenda stormed in.

"Mommy!" The twins scrambled from the table excitedly.

"Brenda!"

"Hello, my little sweeties," Brenda said, gathering the twins in her arms affectionately. "Did you miss Mommy?"

"Yeah, yeah," they chorused, tumbling over each other to get their arms wrapped around her neck.

"Brenda! What are you doing home today? I didn't expect you until late tomorrow afternoon," Erin said with surprise. "Where's Nathan?"

"Don't mention that man's name to me!" Brenda's face was furious now. "I never want to see him again!"

"What? What in the world's going on—"

"Where's Daddy?" Huntley stopped squeezing her neck and showering her face with kisses long enough to remember his father.

"Uh—he'll probably be along anytime," Brenda hedged, drawing him back to her for another round of hugs and kisses.

"He gonna have to paddle Huntwey, Mommy. He's been a bad boy," Holly told her mother primly. "But *I've* been good."

"Have they been bad?" Brenda glanced up at Erin worriedly.

"No. Just normal five-year-olds." Erin was thankful that she had always been a tactful person. It came in unusually handy at the moment.

All of a sudden Brenda's face clouded. She buried it in her hands and started to bawl like a baby.

The twins immediately puckered up and looked very close to tears themselves as Erin hurried over to Brenda and put her arms around her. "Brenda, my goodness, what's the matter?"

"It's that darn, infuriating—pigheaded Nathan!" She sobbed wildly, losing all control now.

"Have you had a quarrel?" Erin bit her tongue, thinking how stupid that must sound! It was apparent that Brenda and Nathan were not on the best of terms at present.

"Yesss!" She sobbed pitifully.

The twins set up a loud howl as they fell around their mother's neck again, confused and frightened by her tears.

"Good lord, what's going on down here?" Price asked as he walked into the bawling, sobbing, puzzled foursome.

"Oh, Price," Erin said, running over to him, whispering worriedly. "I think Brenda and Nathan have had a terrible argument."

"Where's Nathan?" Price glanced around the kitchen.

"Beats me. Brenda arrived here alone a few minutes ago."

155

"Hey, you guys." Price walked over and untangled the twins from Brenda's neck while Erin tried to console their mother. "Let's go over and see if Michael can play for a while." He picked a child up in each arm and started toward the door. "Be right back, Auntie Ewin."

As the door closed behind him, Erin sat Brenda down in a chair and poured her a cup of strong coffee. "Now, Brenda, calm down and tell me what's happened."

Brenda dissolved in a fresh round of tears. "This has been the most miserable week of my life! Nathan and I have done nothing but fight since we left."

Erin couldn't believe her ears. Brenda and Nathan fighting? They couldn't! They had a perfect marriage!

"I thought we would spend the whole week together, just the two of us, one long romantic week. But that—that —jackass has done nothing but gripe and grumble all blessed week long, totally ignoring me!"

"But where *is* Nathan?" Erin persisted worriedly.

"How do I know? I drove off and left him standing at the last gas station we stopped at." Brenda sniffed haughtily.

"Brenda! You didn't!" Erin was astounded.

"I certainly did! I warned him if he barked at me one more time, I would come home by myself!" Brenda blew her nose loudly.

This was absolutely ridiculous. Brenda and Nathan, who always got along so beautifully, were nearly in the divorce courts over his barking at her? Erin shook her head wonderingly. What was this world coming to?

"You just drove off and left him standing in—in—"

"Arkansas."

"Arkansas!" Erin groaned. "You surely didn't!"

"You're lucky, Erin. You're *so* lucky that you're not married and have to put up with a stubborn man every day of your life." She blew her nose loudly again. "I have *had it* with Nathan Daniels!"

"Now, Brenda, you don't mean that. You love Nathan —"

"I know I do!" she gulped in a childish voice before dissolving in a new round of tears. "But I don't *like* him!"

"Oh, good grief, will you stop it!" Erin wet a paper towel and wiped Brenda's flushed and puffy face. "Please calm down."

"What's Price doing here?" she said with a hiccup, gratefully letting Erin mother her. "Do you know Price?"

"We've met." Boy, have we met, Erin thought ironically. "He stopped by to visit with you and Nathan a few days ago and . . . oh, it's too long a story to go into now, Brenda. I'll tell you all about it when you're more—later."

Brenda clutched Erin's hand frantically. "Don't ever marry, Erin! All husbands are nothing but—rat finks!"

"Brenda, you can't mean that! You and Nathan have a wonderful marriage."

"We did—up until this week. Oh, Erin, I'm so miserable!" She laid her head down on the kitchen table and cried.

Erin patted her head absently, wondering how poor Nathan was going to get home from Arkansas.

Price opened the back door and stepped into the kitchen. "Cathy said the twins could stay over there for a while." He glanced nervously at the woman sobbing helplessly in the chair. "Everything all right here?"

"Just ducky," Erin said with a shaky smile. "Brenda never wants to see her rat finky husband again, and he's standing somewhere in Arkansas trying to hitchhike his way back home."

"Ohhhh—he's not going to get away with this!" Brenda declared angrily, pushing her chair back from the table. "Nathan—stubborn, mule-headed Daniels is not going to get away with this!" She stomped heatedly out of the kitchen, muttering vilely under her breath.

Price grinned at Erin. "Somehow I get the distinct feeling that the perfect marriage has soured."

"You don't have to look so gleeful, Price. Brenda is really mad at him!"

Price's smile faded slowly. "Yeah, I know. What should we do?"

"I'm worried about Nathan," Erin confessed. "She left him standing at a gas station somewhere in Arkansas!"

"Damn!" Price whistled low. "That's a rotten thing to do."

Erin glanced at him sharply. "It was his fault! He crabbed at her all week!"

"And I suppose she was perfect all week?" He crossed his arms arrogantly.

"Men! They *always* stick together," Erin said disgustedly. "So what do you think we should do? Maybe you should drive toward Arkansa—"

Erin was interrupted by Brenda entering the kitchen once more, dragging two heavy suitcases behind her. "*If* you should happen to see *your* friend, tell him he's moved!" She threw the suitcases at Price's feet and huffed angrily back out of the kitchen.

"Oh, brother!" Price groaned. "This is one hell of a mess!"

"Look, Price, there's a bread truck pulling up in the drive." Erin glanced out the window anxiously.

Price leaned over her shoulder and mumbled glumly. "Well, brace yourself. It looks like the rat fink has hitched a ride home—and he doesn't look too happy. I'd better go out and break the news to him that he no longer resides here."

Price let himself out through the back screen door, a worried frown on his handsome features. Erin could hear him and Nathan talking to each other, Nathan raising his voice angrily at times.

"He's here, isn't he?" Brenda hissed from the doorway.

Erin turned around, startled, to face her. "I didn't hear you come back! Yes, Nathan just drove up a few minutes ago. Do you want me and Price to leave—"

"No! I don't ever want to see that man again!" she hissed shrilly in a loud whisper. "Promise me you won't leave me here alone, Erin. Promise!"

"Brenda, don't start crying again!" Erin warned with a trace of impatience creeping into her voice. "I'm not going anywhere." She was beginning to grow a little tired of Brenda's theatrics.

"What are they saying? Is Nathan upset?"

"Wouldn't *you* be if you just rode in from Arkansas in a bread truck?"

"Oh . . . he'll probably kill me!" Brenda said, wringing her hands and peering over Erin's shoulder anxiously.

"He's not going to kill you, but that *was* pretty rotten, Brenda!"

"He deserved it," she muttered defensively. "Oh, look! He's starting toward the house! What should I do? Tell him he can't come in, Erin!"

"I can't tell him he can't come in!" Erin said exasperatedly. "It's his house!"

"Then we'll leave! Come on, Erin, let's get out of here before I blow my top again."

Erin sighed defeatedly as Brenda pulled her toward the door. How did she get herself into messes like this?

They passed the two men in practically a dead run on the way to Erin's car. Erin smiled sheepishly as she encountered a puzzled Price. "We're leaving."

"Brenda Daniels, I want to talk to you—" Nathan's face turned an angry red as he reached out to capture his wife's fleeing form.

"Well, I don't want to talk to you, you—heel!" She broke his grasp and ran for the car, sobbing furiously.

"Brenda . . . damn it!"

"Nathan, maybe it's best if you let her alone until she

159

cools off," Erin said gently. "I'll try to talk some sense into her."

"Would you?" Nathan looked relieved and tired. "I don't know what the hell has gotten into her this week. She's been as cranky as an old bear!"

Erin and Price smiled at each other. Now where had they heard that recently? "Don't worry," Erin said consolingly, patting Nathan on the arm reassuringly. "I'll take care of everything."

"How do you figure a woman?" Nathan mumbled to Price as Erin turned and walked away. "If Erin manages to calm that hellcat down, it will be a miracle!"

"Oh, don't worry," Price said absently as he watched the red VW fade into the distance. "Erin will get that hellish streak out of her." He turned and gave Nathan an encouraging grin. "If nothing else, Erin's driving will scare it out of her!"

"Don't you think we should stop somewhere?" Erin pleaded wearily. "We've driven for hours!"

Brenda dried her eyes for what seemed like the hundredth time and looked at Erin pathetically. "I don't care what we do."

"Are you hungry?"

"No." She sobbed loudly.

"Thirsty? Don't you at least need to go to the bathroom?" Erin searched for any plausible excuse to stop the car.

"I don't care, Erin! Do anything you want to, but I'm not going back home!" she warned with a large hiccup.

Naturally! Erin fumed silently. So far she had been extremely unsuccessful in bringing Brenda to her senses.

In another twenty minutes Erin impatiently pulled into a truck stop and shut the motor off. "I am going to at least have a cup of coffee!" She got out of the car and walked into the café, hoping that Brenda would follow. This was to have been a nice, quiet day with a picnic, laughter, an eagerly awaited romantic evening with Price . . . Suddenly she resented Brenda very much.

Brenda came dragging in behind Erin, lamenting dramatically as they sat down opposite each other in a booth, "Why is life so cruel?"

"Why is there air?" Erin said, sounding more surly than she intended. "I don't know the answer to your question, Brenda, but I honestly think you are blowing this argument all out of proportion."

"You don't understand, Erin." Brenda stared morosely at the ceiling. "Nathan used to spend hours alone with me. He used to tell me over and over again how much he loved me, how pretty I was, how he couldn't live without me."

"And he doesn't anymore?"

"Well . . . yes . . . occasionally, but not like he used to!"

Erin gave the waitress their order, then turned back to Brenda. "Nathan loves you very much, Brenda. Don't you think that a couple just naturally tends to take the other for granted after they've been married as long as you and Nathan have?"

"They shouldn't," Brenda shot back irritably.

"I know, but they do," Erin returned quietly. "I don't think that means that Nathan loves you any less than the day he married you. Do you tell him how much you love him every day, how you can't live without him?"

Brenda was quiet for a moment. "Not every day. But he knows I do. I love him, Erin, more than anything in the world," she admitted in a small, childish voice.

"I know you do," Erin said tenderly. "And he loves you just as much."

"He'll probably never speak to me again after what I did to him this morning." She let out a weak giggle. "You should have seen the look on his face when I pulled out of the gas station!"

"I can imagine."

161

"Oh, I've made such a mess of things, Erin." Brenda gave a long, shuddering sigh. "Don't ever give your love to a man," she warned again sadly.

"You don't think it's worth it?" Erin asked, thinking of last night in Price's strong arms. The point in question was beside the fact now. Her heart had already been given. "You don't think you'd miss having a man to come home to you each evening, a man whose arms you can lie in at night, someone to tell your problems to at the end of each day, someone to share your life with? I can't believe you'd want to give that up, Brenda."

Tears had begun to slip silently down Brenda's cheeks now. "No, I don't want to give that up."

"No marriage can be perfect." Erin stopped for a moment and laughed ironically. "Listen to me! I'm the one who's been looking for the perfect marriage, determined to settle for nothing less!"

"Nathan's and mine is nearly perfect," Brenda said, a little life creeping back into her voice now. "Oh, we have our fights, but most of the time I wouldn't trade my marriage for a million dollars."

"That's what I've been trying to tell Price, but he won't believe it!" Erin laughed again.

"Price?" Brenda took a sip of the coffee the waitress had brought. "Is there something going on between you and Price?"

"I don't know, Brenda. I try to tell myself there isn't . . . at least, nothing serious, but. . . ."

"I didn't think Price would be ready for another commitment so soon after Jean—"

"Jeannie? I know all about her," Erin confessed tiredly.

"To be truthful, I didn't think *you* would be ready for one so soon after Quinn."

Erin shrugged her shoulders. "I didn't, either. Maybe I'm not. Then again, maybe I am. Anyway, that's all beside the point. Price has an opportunity to go back to Jeannie. He may take it."

"Surely not!" Brenda gasped indignantly. "She really dumped on that poor man!"

"Well, then I can only surmise he enjoys being dumped on, because her new love affair fell flat and she called him this week. They even saw each other."

"Men! Aren't they disgusting! Well, you're not just going to sit there and let her have him again, are you?"

"What can I do? After all, we didn't even know each other until five days ago!"

"Oh, but you did! Don't you remember—you thought he was a living doll at our wedding!"

"When I was that age, Brenda, I thought *anything* that wore pants was a living doll! No, I barely remember meeting him."

"Well, he remembers you. Every once in a while he used to ask me where you were and if we were still good friends."

"No kidding?" Erin sat up to face her. "I wonder why."

"I heard him tell Nathan one day he thought you were a good-lookin' chick, and he'd like to—" Brenda blushed. "Well, they didn't know I was listening, and you know how blunt men can be sometimes," she excused embarrassedly.

Erin's smile was radiant. Price had thought of her in the most intimate way years ago! This was absolutely wonderful! And that was *before* Jeannie! "I know!" Erin agreed happily, absently stirring five tablespoons of sugar into her coffee. "Extremely blunt!"

"I'm exhausted," Brenda admitted with a yawn. "Let's finish our coffee, then we can go back home. I'm going to make all this up to Nathan tonight."

"Well, I should hope so. . . ."

"Excuse me, ladies," a brawny-looking man said, walking up to their table as he wiped the sweat off his brow with a grimy handkerchief. "Do one of you chicks own that red VW sitting out in front?"

"That chick does," Brenda said, pointing at Erin.

Erin shot her an exasperated glare.

"Well, there's a feller out there that said to tell whoever owned it that they got a flat." He stuffed the soiled handkerchief back into his pocket.

"Oh, darn it! That's all I need now," Erin said and groaned, trying to see the VW out one of the truck stop windows but failing. "Is there someone around who can change it for me?"

"I don't know. You'll have to ask," he replied as he calmly walked away from the table and pounced on one of the empty bar stools at the counter.

"Why didn't you ask *him* to fix it?" Brenda suggested worriedly.

"I thought he would offer to," Erin said in a disgusted voice as she watched the man from the corner of her eye unconcernedly order a cup of coffee and a piece of pie. "Let's go see if we can find someone to change it for us."

They slid out of the booth and walked to the register to pay their bill, both of them feeling painfully self-conscious of being two girls alone in a truck stop. Other than the waitress, the café was filled with men.

"Have I got a hole in my jeans?" Brenda whispered, clinging to Erin's small form.

"No, have I?"

"Get a load of the way that man on the third bar stool is looking at us," she muttered uneasily under her breath.

Erin nonchalantly let her eyes rove down the row of seats and linger for a moment on the gorilla who was sitting on the third seat. She smiled weakly as his face broke into a wide, licentious grin, exposing two yellow gold teeth and one rotten one.

"Oh, lord! Let's get out of here!" Erin forced herself to

164

smile brightly at the big brute as she and Brenda nearly tripped over each other in their haste to exit.

They tumbled out the front door and rounded the building, heading for the spot where they had parked the VW. "I hope that man doesn't decide to follow us," Brenda said, fretting. "If he does, you stall him while I run for help—" Brenda's voice broke off in a scream as one arm came out from behind the VW and literally jerked her off her feet.

Erin's heart nearly stopped as she felt someone grab her from behind and pull her up against a broad wall of a chest. One large hand closed over her mouth as she started to scream at the top of her lungs.

"Shhhh—you want to bring the cops down on us?"

"Price!"

His hands loosened on her mouth and he spun her around to face him. "You called?"

"Price Seaver! You dirty—"

"Now wait a minute, this wasn't *my* idea. It was all Nathan's," Price said quickly. "I was for coming in there and carrying you out of the restaurant like a man, but Nathan wanted to do it a little quieter."

"Why didn't you just let us know you were here?" she sputtered, still trying to convince her legs to support her. Her heart was beating like a jackhammer from the fright he had just given her.

"Oh, sure. With Brenda in the mood she's in!"

Erin looked around frantically. "Where is Brenda?" All Erin had heard was Brenda's terrified scream shortly before Price had grabbed her.

"Nathan took her to their car. I think the lovebirds need to talk." He grinned as the sound of flying gravel and tires squealing on pavement reached their ears.

"And you had to go to these drastic means?" She gasped, prying his hands away from her waist angrily.

"It worked, didn't it?" He looked extremely proud of

himself at the moment. "Darn. Give us a little credit. It took us three hours to find your car—and cost fifty dollars to get that guy to tell you your car had a flat!"

"Price, you are horrible!" Erin scolded with a relieved laugh.

"Yeah, I know it." He cringed at the sound of Brenda's voice screaming one last time as Nathan pulled out of the truck stop. "Ah! Ain't love grand!"

"They really do love each other." She smiled tenderly at him, wanting to kiss him so badly she ached.

"It sounds like it," he agreed blandly. "Come here, troll, and give me a kiss."

Erin went into his arms happily and they exchanged a long, lazy kiss.

"How did you ever find us?" she finally managed to ask.

"Drove into every café and truck stop for the last fifty miles." He kissed her on the tip of her nose playfully.

"How nice. But why all the bother? I would have brought Brenda home later."

"I missed having our picnic today," he whispered huskily as their mouths merged again. "And I was determined I wasn't going to miss our date tonight."

"You sound like you might be takin' a likin' to plain little ole trollish me," Erin teased in a hillbilly twang.

"Naw. Never! Nathan and I drew straws and he got the good-looking, ravishing doll, and I got the troll." He sighed disappointedly, brushing his lips across hers tantalizingly.

"I don't believe you for one minute! I happen to know for a fact that you noticed me at Brenda and Nathan's wedding all those years ago. You've even asked Brenda about me occasionally," she revealed smugly.

"Now who's been feeding you all that bull? I've never looked at an ugly, homely girl like you in my whole life." He winked and pinched her on the fanny.

"Just what *did* you tell Nathan you'd like to do to me?

Brenda said she overheard you and Nathan talking one day—"

Price stopped her with a masterful kiss. When she was finally able to catch her breath, she asked again, "What did you tell him?"

"Promise you won't get mad." He grinned cockily.

"I won't get mad."

He leaned over and pulled her up against his long male length and rubbed against her suggestively as he whispered in her ear.

"Good heavens, Price! You *are* unbelievable!"

"I know. I really can be when I put my heart into it!" he said proudly, his hand lazily stroking her back. "Come on, I passed a little motel about ten miles down the road where we can check in and I'll prove it," he murmured against the silken mass of her hair.

"Don't be silly. We're not going to spend the night in a motel. . . ." Her voice trailed off weakly as his hand caressed the side of her breast.

"Why not?" He kissed her slowly. "I want to hold you in my arms again, kiss you, touch you, have you touch me the way we did last night."

Erin felt her defenses crumbling fast as he pleaded against her mouth softly. "What's wrong with a man wanting to be with his woman?" he whispered persuasively.

His woman! That sounded so very, very wonderful. Had it only been a phrase that popped into his head, or did he realize what he had said? At the moment it made very little difference to her. She loved him, and that was all that mattered. The smoldering flame that she saw in his eyes comforted her. Price Seaver was a doomed man—doomed to a lifetime with her—only she wasn't about to tell him so right now. She sighed, running her hands through the thick hair on his broad chest. She'd let him discover that all by himself.

Parting her lips, she raised her mouth to meet his kisses as his hands continued to explore her soft body. So much love and warmth seemed to flow between them at the moment that it held them both in awe.

"Don't you think we'd better go before we make a public spectacle of ourselves?" he urged in an unsteady voice, his eyes growing dark and slumbrous with desire.

He reached behind him and opened the car door, his mouth never leaving hers for an instant. Together they got in and he pulled her over close on the seat as he started the engine.

"Can you drive with both of us in one seat?" she asked between his long lazy kisses. A strange feeling of languor began to invade her body.

"If I can't, we'll walk the rest of the way," he promised in a ragged breath.

They drove to the motel exchanging heated kisses, their growing need for each other causing a sense of urgency in them, yet each one wanting to prolong the inevitable as long as possible. Erin wanted to touch him, to explore every inch of this man she loved. She wanted to kiss him, to feel his naked skin next to hers, to hear his voice raggedly pleading for more.

Although the ride took only ten minutes, to Erin it seemed like ten hours. As the door swung shut in the small motel room Price had rented, he scooped her up in his arms and carried her to the bed, then laid her down gently. Her breathing quickened and her cheeks became warm as he began slowly to undress her, kissing each naked area as her clothes fell away. His emerald green gaze moved over her feminine loveliness, and his breathing deepened to match hers.

"Shouldn't we close the blinds—there's so much light in here," she protested weakly as his mouth found its way home to hers once more.

"Maybe we'd better," he agreed huskily as his hands

lovingly traced the curve of her hip, "but we're going to turn on a light. I want to see my beautiful troll when I make love to her."

"Do you really find me beautiful?" she asked in awe.

Price pulled away from her long enough to meet her eyes, his serious gaze telling her all she needed to know. "That's about the silliest question you've ever asked me. Of course I find you beautiful. I always have."

"I think you're very beautiful, too—" She laughed at his instant frown. "Well, you know what I mean."

"No. Why don't you show me." He grinned back, reaching over to close the blinds and switch on the lamp next to the bed.

Her hands reached out and methodically began to unbutton his shirt as she whispered softly against his mouth, "I may not do this as well as you do, but I think you're *very* handsome." Her hands stroked his broad chest, her finger trailing playfully down the thin line of dark hair that ran below his trousers. "I love the sexy way you look with your shirt off. . . ."

"You noticed?"

"I noticed."

"Do go on," he urged. "I could listen to this all night long."

"Well, I love the color of your eyes. . . ."

"You hate men with green eyes. Your words, not mine," he said teasingly, kissing her tenderly.

"And I love the color of your hair, and the way your skin tastes after we've made love . . . and I love the way you go all limp when I kiss you here—and here—and here—"

Price groaned, his breathing growing heavier.

"And I think your legs are incredibly cute," she continued as she helped him slip out of his pants and underwear, discarding them in a heap on the floor. She ran her hands lightly over his legs, touching and savoring the feel of his long, muscular length against her bare flesh. "I love the size of your hands. Do you know that one of your hands would make two of mine?" She picked up his hand and kissed it reverently. "I love the way your hands touch me, all soft and gentle, yet firm and knowledgeable."

Taking her hand, he guided it to himself, moaning pleasurably as her touch sent shivers of delight coursing through his body. His kisses grew hungry, then demanding as the gathering twilight filtered through the tiny room.

"Make me your man, Erin Holmes," he urged passionately.

Suddenly they could no longer control their overpowering need for each other and they became lost in an outpouring of fiery sensations, each giving deep and loving pleasure to the other. His kisses sent a wild torrent of desire racing through her as he moved his large body to cover her smaller one. The flames of passion burned within both of them as he entered her, and they moved together slowly at first. Then the dam opened and she surrendered completely to his lovemaking, striving to show him her overwhelming need for him, just how much she loved his touch, the feel of him, the musky male scent of him.

They didn't want to yield to the burning sweetness that seemed captive within them. They both fought to stave off the inevitable, but all too soon they were caught up in a bursting blaze of sensations. She gasped in sweet agony as he moaned softly, their pleasure pure and explosive. Price cried out her name as they both reached their fulfillment simultaneously, his embrace tightening almost painfully before he fell limp beside her.

Slowly they drifted back to earth and she snuggled close in his arms. She could never remember feeling as peaceful, content and satisfied as she did now. For the first time she realized that Quinn Daniels had only been a foolish young girl's dream. She had never loved Quinn with the awesome, overpowering certainty that she now felt for Price Seaver.

Burying her face against the corded muscles of his chest, she spoke first. "I suppose that what I've been trying to say is, most of all, I love *you,* Price."

The room was quiet; only the sounds of the passing traffic outside shattered the stillness occasionally. Price didn't speak for a few moments, but when he did, his voice was soft but not alarming. "I don't know what to say, Erin. I'm afraid"—his voice broke with huskiness—"this has all happened so fast. . . ."

"I know." She patted his chest reassuringly. "I know. I'm not asking for anything, Price. I just wanted you to know that I love you."

Reclaiming her lips, he crushed her to him almost painfully, her calm shattered by the hunger of his kisses once more. His kisses became heated, almost angry at times as he made love to her again almost savagely, yet with incredible tenderness. As wave after wave of ecstasy washed over them, they cried out each other's names, clinging to one another helplessly as the world spun crazily, then finally slowed, then returned to normal.

It was hours later when they finally drifted off to sleep in each other's arms. Tomorrow she would go home. If Price decided he wanted her, she would be waiting for him. It might take a week, a month, a lifetime, but her perfect man would come for her, she reminded herself tearfully. Well, maybe not perfect, but Price *would* come for her! He simply had to. Love, will you ever remember me, was her last coherent question as she dropped off into a numbed, peaceful sleep.

CHAPTER TEN

"I still say you're being a silly fool." Brenda sat on the bed and watched Erin pack the remaining articles of her clothing, then close the lid and snap the lock shut. "Are you even listening to me?"

"Yes, but you're not saying anything," Erin replied calmly.

"How can you be so serene about all this! If you love Price, how can you just let him get in his car and drive back to—to that woman!"

Erin sighed tiredly. "First of all, there is nothing in the world that I could do to prevent it. Second, I don't know for certain that he *is* going back to Jeannie, and third, all he would have to do is ask me for some type of commitment—which he isn't about to do—and then I'd gladly say yes. But, as you can plainly see, I seem to be butting my head against a brick wall."

"Well, you *know* he cares for you, Erin! You spent the night with him last night, didn't you?" Brenda asked.

Erin's face turned a warm pink. "No—Price rented me a separate—"

"Oh, come on!"

"All right! Yes! I spent the night with him So what? It's my business. I'm over twenty-one," Erin defended weakly.

Brenda lay back across the bed and stared up at the ceiling dreamily. "I hope he was as wonderful, as exciting, as passionate as my darling Nathan was."

Erin looked at her friend warily. "Darling Nathan? You seem to have changed your tune since we last discussed that—uh—I believe rat fink was the term you used."

"But that was yesterday and this is today!" Brenda said brightly. "He managed to sway my opinion of him to a more favorable one."

"Well," Erin said as she glanced around the room one last time, "I should be on my way. I'd like to get home before too late."

"You're being foolish," Brenda warned once more as she followed Erin out the bedroom door. "You're going to be sorry!"

"I usually am," her friend agreed.

As they reached the kitchen, where Price and Nathan sat having a cup of coffee, Price stood and took her bag from her hand.

"Hi. All ready?"

"All ready." Erin smiled at him affectionately. They had said practically nothing to each other since they came home this morning.

"I'll walk to the car with you." Price's gaze met hers for a moment, then skipped away quickly.

Erin kneeled and hugged the twins, giggling delightedly as they showered her face with sloppy kisses. "You make Mommy bring you up to visit with me soon. We'll take an afternoon and go to the zoo. Would you like that?"

"Sure!" they replied enthusiastically.

The entire Daniels family escorted Erin and Price out to the small VW, much to both their dismay. Erin had desperately wanted a few minutes alone with Price. Not that she expected anything to come out of those few minutes, but at least she would be able to kiss him good-bye in private.

"You dwive careful in this kwackerbox," Holly cautioned in an adult tone. "This kwar just doesn't wook vewy safe to me!"

Everyone laughed as Erin got in behind the wheel. "I will, Holly. You can count on it."

Price and Erin looked at each other anxiously.

"Oh . . . hey." Nathan suddenly remembered the circumstances. "Why don't we go into the house and find something to eat. I'm starving."

"Hungry! Nathan you couldn't be—" Brenda saw the distress signal Nathan shot her with his eyes. "Oh! Yes, well . . . you didn't eat your dessert. Come on, kids," she said, leaning in the car and kissing Erin on the cheek. "Call me!"

"I will. See you later." Erin hugged her.

Price leaned on the car window frame for a moment, an uneasy silence settling over the couple as the Daniels family ran back toward the house, laughing noisily.

"How long will it take you to drive home?" His eyes finally found hers.

"Just an hour or so. It depends on the traffic. When are you leaving?"

"As soon as you pull out of the drive. I have a good six-hour drive ahead of me."

"That will make it very late when you get home then." Erin gazed back at him lovingly.

"Yeah, it will. I think I love you, too, Erin."

Erin's mouth dropped open. "What?"

"I said—I think I love you, too, Erin—but I want us both to be very sure this time." His eyes were tender as he picked up her hand and stroked it gently. "Let's give ourselves some time away from each other. Time to assess things in a new light. I can't seem to think straight when you're with me or when you're in my arms. . . ." His voice was soft and deep as he stared at her for many long moments.

"All right, Price, how long? A week, a month—a year?" Erin agreed softly.

"However long it takes. We'll both know when the time

is right." He put his hand under her chin, turning her toward him. "Right now I want to kiss you, lovely lady, but if I do, I'll never let you out of this drive." One long finger gently traced the outline of her troubled features. "Wait for me, Erin."

"I will, but don't take too long, Price. I've waited twenty-five years to find you. I need you."

"We should know within a month," he said quietly, a promise shining in his eyes.

Erin reached down and turned the key to start the engine. "I'd better be going." She was fighting tears that threatened to overtake her. The last thing she wanted was to make him feel pressed into a commitment he wasn't ready to make.

"I'll be seeing you, Erin Holmes."

"I'll be waiting, Price Seaver."

Tears were nearly blinding her as she backed her car out of the drive and started for home. One month! He had said one month. But did he mean it? If he really loved her, he would know now. It wouldn't take a month.

As the red car sped steadily toward home, Erin knew without a doubt that she loved him. She sighed deeply. Maybe women knew these things quicker than men did. Maybe it was because women matured faster than men did. Maybe it was something in their genes. Erin shook herself mentally. Maybe it was because she was such a stupid fool and fell in love with the wrong man again! Whatever the reason, she would know in a month. If Price lucked out and her knight in shining armor didn't show up sooner and whisk her off to blissville! She wasn't going to be stupid enough to wait around forever for him. She could spare a month—but that was all.

It was late afternoon when Erin pulled into her own garage. Reaching down to turn off the ignition, she leaned her head on the steering wheel in weary gratitude. It felt good to be back home.

The apartment was dusty after being neglected for a week, so she went right to work. Two hours later everything was clean once more. It was considerably easier to work without four additional chubby hands helping. Once again her mind traveled back to Price's words this afternoon. Could she bear to wait a month for him? Would life be worth living the next month without the feel of his arms around her, the touch of his mouth, being able to look into that lazy, slumbrous green-eyed gaze of his? For her it wouldn't be. And what if the unthinkable should happen and he went back to Jeannie?

Erin suddenly felt tears streaming down her cheeks and dropping off her nose in rivers. Here she was, crying over a man again! All the promises, all the vows she had made to herself were as useless as the tears that fell steadily down the front of her blouse.

Well, she would go after him. If he didn't come in a month—maybe three weeks—she would shamelessly go to Memphis and . . . and . . . and what?

With a tired sigh of resignation, she buried her face in her hands and cried for hours.

By ten o'clock she was tired, tearless and hungry. Deciding to have a pizza delivered, she phoned in her order, then took her bath quickly. By the time she had blown her hair dry, the doorbell rang. "Mercy, that was fast!" she thought, reaching for her money and hurrying toward the door.

When she opened it, her heart nearly stopped. Instead of a pizza delivery boy standing before her, it was a tall, brown-haired man with the most lovely green eyes she had ever seen. He was holding a large bouquet of roses and carrying three packages wrapped in Christmas paper.

Erin caught her breath and leaned against the doorjamb, her heart suddenly feeling very light and happy. With an amused grin she asked, "Yes?"

"Excuse me, ma'am. Does Erin Holmes live here?" the man asked indifferently.

"Yes, she does. Who wants to know?"

"I'm here to deliver one knight in shining armor, one perfect husband, these flowers"—he shoved the bouquet into her hand unceremoniously—"and three Christmas presents. Does she accept?"

"Well, now, that depends." Erin crossed her arms arrogantly and surveyed the "knight" suspiciously.

"On what?" came the sexy reply.

"On who's sending them."

He reached out and kissed her tenderly. "Price Seaver, ma'am."

"Oh." Erin smiled at him sweetly. "Sorry, but there's some mistake. He's not due for another month!" she said, then slammed the door in his startled face.

"Erin!" Price pounded on the door loudly. "Open this door, woman. I would have been here earlier, sweetheart, but my damn horse threw me in the forest and I almost never got back on the stupid thing!"

Gales of laughter erupted from Erin as tears ran freely down her face. Price was here! He had come after her. Her knight in shining armor had finally shown up!

The door swung back open and she was in his arms, laughing, crying, kissing, her salty tears mixing with his.

"Oh, Erin, sweetheart. I knew five minutes after you left that you were the only woman I wanted in my life." His kisses were a hungry reaffirmation of his love for her. "I may not be the perfect husband, but I'm damn sure going to work hard at it."

"Oh, Price. I don't want a perfect marriage! All I want is to spend the rest of my life as your wife. For me, that *will* be the perfect marriage!"

"Help me get into the apartment," he murmured between heated kisses. "Your neighbors will have a field day with this!"

Erin had completely forgotten she was standing out in the hall locked in a passionate embrace with Price. "Oh, darling, I couldn't care less. But maybe we should go in," she agreed as the woman across the hall opened her door and glared at Erin.

They kissed their way into the apartment and sank down on the sofa together. Erin took the Christmas packages from his hands and laid them on the coffee table.

Turning back to him, she gave Price a wicked grin. "Now, let me see. I always dreamed what I would do to my knight when he finally showed up." She winked at him broadly. "Just sit back and enjoy this, knighty. I'm going to do something I've fantasized about since I reached puberty!"

"Hallelujah! So you are *that* kind of woman!" Price groaned pleasurably as she swiftly rid him of his shirt and everything else he was wearing.

They walked to the bedroom and lay on the bed, kissing with reckless abandon as their bodies melted against each other's. She felt her breasts crush against the hardness of his chest as her hands explored his body lovingly, exulting in the familiar smell of him.

"I was so afraid I'd have to wait a month—one long month—before I could kiss you again," she confessed as his mouth moved along the dusky peaks of her breasts, outlining them with the tip of his tongue.

"That was about as stupid as my asking you to be my friend," Price agreed with a low gasp as her hand found him intimately.

"You changed your mind again? We're not friends anymore?" Erin caressed him gently.

"No, from now on we're strictly lovers," he murmured, taking her mouth hungrily with his. His hand searched out the pleasure points of her body, teasing her senses to throbbing awareness.

"I haven't heard you say the words yet, Price," she whispered urgently. "You haven't said—"

"I love you? I *love* you, my beautiful, adorable little troll. There must be at least a hundred different ways to say I love you, Erin, and if you give me your love, I'll find the way to say them all to you," he vowed adamantly, kissing her with every sentence.

"And you're not still mad at me because I fried your beautiful fish—"

"I said I loved you, sweetheart, I didn't say I'd lost my memory! I could still wring your neck every time I think about—"

"I'll make it up to you," she promised, hurriedly kissing him in a way that took his mind off the subject.

"You'd better," he told her huskily as he pulled her on top of him. "I'm going to make you apologize to me at least twice a day in this manner," he pulled her tighter against him, "for the next year."

"Oh, my goodness," she said in mock despair. "Why, I'll *simply* die!"

"Yeah, but what a way to go!" He grinned.

"Gee, since you've doled out such severe punishment, maybe I should get started on my sentence. Now let's see, do I conduct myself in the standard procedures, or should I get aggressive, wanton, wild. . . ."

"Yeah-h-h-h, all of the above," he agreed in a languid tone as her fingers and hands miraculously found all the places that pleased and excited him. "Let's just love each other for the rest of our lives, and enjoy it," he murmured tenderly, his mouth closing sweetly over hers again.

She knew the flooding of uncontrolled joy as she lay in his arms. At last love had remembered her! In a most wondrous and fulfilling way.

Restlessly Price's hands wandered down her sides, skimming her body, drawing her upward to meet his overpowering need of her. Her whole being flooded with desire for the man she so dearly loved as they came together in an act as old as time. Their bodies vibrated with liquid fire for each other as he became one with her. All else ceased to exist in the world as together they poured out their love for each other in murmured words, with heated touches, and finally anguished cries of emotion as they scaled the top of the mountain and slid passionately over.

"Oh, my lovely Erin, I love you so much," Price said in a low, throaty voice when he was able to speak once more.

Erin's eyes grew serious. "I want you to love me, Price. More than anyone or anything in this world. I won't smother you with that love, but I do want to feel secure in it."

His steady gaze bore into her silent expectation. "I told you once before, Erin, I'm a one-woman man. You can trust your love to me without ever fearing that I'll do anything to destroy it. I think that in some ways what Quinn and Jeannie put us through will strengthen our marriage. We know now when love is good, and when it's all wrong. We're lucky. We found each other, and our love *is* good, Erin."

They exchanged a kiss of mutual love, still wrapped tightly in each other's arms.

Later—much, much later—they lay together in each other's arms, their bodies still moist from their lovemaking. Price refused to loosen his hold on her as he kissed her lazily, his hand gently stroking the crests of each breast.

"How long was it after you left that you realized it was the real thing?" he whispered against the perfume of her hair.

"Days before."

Price raised up on his elbow and looked at her. "Are you serious?"

"Yes, I'm serious. I think I fell in love with you the night you carried me into the bathroom and sat by while I heaved my socks up." Her hand ran lightly through the thick hair on his chest. "But then again, it might have been the next morning, when I saw you in bed and noticed your incredibly sexy, hairy chest. . . ." She recaptured his mouth with hers. They kissed hotly for several minutes before she spoke again. "Price, I know that I'm beginning to sound like a broken record, but—"

"But what about Jeannie?" he mocked teasingly.

"Yes! What about Jeannie!"

"What about her?" He crossed his hands behind his head and stared up at the ceiling. "I wished I smoked. This would be the perfect time for a cigarette."

Erin sat up and glared at him angrily. "Will you be serious! I want to know what she said when you gave her your answer!" Erin looked at him suspiciously. "You did give her your answer, didn't you?"

"In the movies it always looks so good when the man lights a cigarette and hands it to the woman. Then they both take a long drag—" His words were interrupted by a pillow hitting him in the face.

Rolling over on her, he captured her flailing hands with his large ones. "All right, if you must know—she took a gun and blew her brains out. Right there in my office. It was disgusting. It took the janitor an hour to get the place back in shape."

"Price," Erin gasped, "you're surely kidding me."

Price grinned down at her, kissing the tip of her nose. "I surely am."

"Did you tell her?" Erin demanded, biting his lip painfully.

"Ouch! Yes, I told her!"

"When?"

"The same day she asked me!"

Erin's face softened. "You mean you didn't even have

181

to think about it? You told her the same day you were in Memphis?"

Price chuckled. "I had thought about it, Erin, constantly for the last six months. I realized that it was over a long time ago." He kissed her again lovingly. "If it makes you feel any better, I never loved her in the way I love you. You're the first woman in my life who ever made me feel the way I do at this moment, Ms. Holmes. I love you very, very much."

"It does make me feel better, Mr. Knight. I love you, too."

"And Quinn?"

"I've forgotten what he even looks like!" she admitted honestly.

"Good, because from now on you're my woman, like it or not!"

"I like it!"

His hand slid down the length of her silken thigh. "Oh, yeah? Prove it." His mouth swooped down to capture hers, forcing her lips open to his thrusting tongue as the peal of the doorbell seeped through their passion-clouded senses.

"Who is that?" Price grumbled disgustedly.

"Pizza man," Erin murmured, bringing his mouth down to meet hers once more. "Oh, my gosh, it's the pizza man!" She scrambled out of bed and fumbled for her robe. "I called for pizza over two hours ago!"

The happy couple sat on her living room couch, kissing and munching contentedly on the pizza.

"This is good." Erin sighed between mouthfuls. "I shouldn't be eating this . . . I *have* to lose ten pounds."

Price frowned at her and took another bite out of his slice. "You shift one ounce of flab around on all those sexy curves and you'll have me to fight."

"No," Erin said firmly, reaching for her third piece. "I

182

mean it. I'm going to go on a diet first thing in the morning. I'm very strong-willed. I can do it if I set my mind to it. Do you want the last piece?"

"No, you eat it."

"Thanks. As I was saying, I'll have this weight off in no time flat." She bit into the last piece and rolled her eyes. "Gosh, this tastes good!"

"Whatever you say. Just so you can get into a wedding dress."

Erin paused in the middle of a bite. "Wedding dress?"

"You know, for a girl who's a born romantic, you're not very curious when your knight in shining armor finally does ride up. Don't you want to know what the fool brought you?"

Erin grinned sweetly. "I thought he already gave it to me. Twice."

"Naughty woman. Now you don't get your Christmas presents."

Erin eyed the gaily wrapped boxes greedily. "Are those really for me?"

"I don't know who else I'd be taking them to at this time of year."

Erin laid her pizza down and scooted closer to him, wrapping her arms around his neck. "But why do I get Christmas presents in August?" She kissed his neck, snuggling against him contentedly.

"Because you're such a troll, Santa probably always flew right over your little house." He reached out and grabbed her hands that were exploring now. "And if you don't stop it, it's going to be another hour before you get to open them."

"I'll stop." Erin ceased her actions after one final intimate pinch. "I want to open the big one first."

Price grinned at her devilishly. "Oh! You mean the box?"

"Price!" She tore into the wrapping excitedly. "How did you know what I wanted?"

"We made out our lists last week, don't you remember?" Price was beaming at her in undisguised love as the paper fell away and she lifted a sable brown full-length mink coat out.

"Oh, Price," she whispered in awe. "You can't be serious."

"I'm very serious, my lovely Erin."

"But it's so expensive—I couldn't take this. . . ."

"You're going to be my wife. You'd better get used to being pampered. I plan on doing a lot of this." He kissed her again. "Now, open the small box next."

Erin's fingers were trembling so, she could hardly get the tiny box unwrapped. Her eyes filled with tears as she opened the lid and a large diamond engagement ring sparkled back at her.

Price reached in and took the ring out of the box and tenderly slipped it on the third finger of her left hand. "We've both waited a long time for this day, Erin. Will you trust the rest of your life to my loving care? I promise you that I'll never give you cause to regret it."

"I would be very happy to be your wife, Price."

"It won't be a perfect marriage, sweetheart, but it will be a damn good one." His voice had an infinitely compassionate tone as his lips met hers in love. Erin leaned against his solid form, giving herself freely up to his love and protection for the rest of her life.

"Now, how about opening that last gift. I would have been here two hours sooner if I hadn't turned the town upside down looking for the last item," Price said minutes later as they broke apart reluctantly.

Erin looked at him and smiled puzzledly. What other gift was there? He had given her a mink coat, a diamond ring, and the promise of a near-perfect marriage. Everything on her gift list. She unwrapped the paper hurriedly and opened the box. Her face lit up in a radiant smile as she surveyed the contents. Her life was now complete!

It was very very late as Erin and Price sat on the sofa, still wrapped in each other's arms.

Four yellow bird slippers stared back at them sightlessly.

"Don't you think we'd better go to bed? It's getting late." Price kissed her softly. "We have a big day ahead of us tomorrow."

"Are you going home?" Erin asked sleepily.

"No, if you don't mind quitting your job suddenly, we're going to find a justice of the peace, get married, spend the next three days making love, then we'll both go home together." He kissed her long and lazily. "But for right now, what do you say we get started on a family of our own?"

"Do you still want five children?"

"At the moment I'd give strong consideration to ten." He nuzzled her neck affectionately.

"And if we have twins?"

Price's lips paused in mid-air. "Twins?"

"It's possible, you know. They run on my father's side of the family."

Price's hands ceased their roaming, a frown forming on his handsome face. "Is there an all-night drugstore open near here?"

Erin grinned. "You're just a little late on your thinking, Uncle Pwice. But don't worry, I've been on the pill for several months," she told him reassuringly.

Price eyed her suspiciously. "Oh?"

"You can get that look off your face, Mr. Seaver. It's under doctor's orders for a small problem I've been having," she said with an outright laugh. "I only have three more to take, then I'm through with them."

"Where are they?" he asked politely as his hands resumed their wandering.

"In my purse. Why?"

"Because before I make love to you again, I'm going to run in there and pour them all down the drain," he replied firmly, slipping her robe off her shoulders and kissing his way down her neck.

"Price!" Erin sputtered against his plundering mouth. "The doctor said—"

"What's three days," he pleaded. "I'm getting older by the minute! I want to make some babies now—tonight!"

"Well, you're simply going to have to wait three more days," she said matter-of-factly, her knees going weak as his mouth trailed down to capture one breast lazily. "Don't you think you could *force* yourself to make the best of the situation and just concentrate on making love to your future wife," she added persuasively as her hands reached over to unbutton his shirt slowly.

Price heaved a long sigh as he stood and gently scooped her up in his arms, bird slippers and all. "Gosh, I'll try, Auntie Ewin," he said with a decidedly wicked grin on his handsome face, "I'm certainly going to try."

LOOK FOR NEXT MONTH'S
CANDLELIGHT ECSTASY ROMANCES ®

Candlelight Ecstasy Romances™

$1.95 each

$2.50 each

Candlelight Ecstasy Romances™

$1.95 each

At your local bookstore or use this handy coupon for ordering:

DELL BOOKS
P.O. BOX 1000, PINE BROOK, N.J. 07058-1000

B218C

Please send me the books I have checked above. I am enclosing $_____ (please add 75c per copy to cover postage and handling). Send check or money order—no cash or C.O.D.s. Please allow up to 8 weeks for shipment

Name _____

Address _____

City _____ State/Zip _____

All-new

Candlelight Newsletter

**An exceptional,
free offer awaits readers
of Dell's incomparable Candlelight Ecstasy and Supreme Romances.**

Subscribe to our all-new CANDLELIGHT NEWSLETTER
and you will receive—at absolutely no cost to you—exciting, ex-
clusive information about today's finest romance novels and nov-
elists. You'll be part of a select group to receive sneak previews of
upcoming Candlelight Romances, well in advance of publication.

You'll also go behind the scenes to "meet" our Ecstasy and
Supreme authors, learning firsthand where they get their
ideas and how they made it to the top. News of author appear-
ances and events will be detailed, as well. And contributions from
the Candlelight editor will give you the inside scoop on how she
makes her decisions about what to publish—and how *you* can try
your hand at writing an Ecstasy or Supreme.

You'll find all this and more in Dell's CANDLELIGHT
NEWSLETTER. And best of all, *it costs you nothing.* That's right!
It's Dell's way of thanking our loyal Candlelight readers and of
adding another dimension to your reading enjoyment.

Just fill out the coupon below, return it to us, and look forward to receiving the first of many CANDLELIGHT NEWS-
LETTERS—overflowing with the kind of excitement that only
enhances our romances!